"If Karl is . . . what you suggest," Anna went on haltingly, "then I may have put you in danger by asking you to help me."

"And what are you doing, Fraulein Anna Becker?" Erik asked, his green eyes on her face, the gold deep within them shimmering.

Changing my life, Anna thought. *Making it what I want.*

"I'm running away from home," she answered.

Erik gave a low whistle. "You don't do things by halves, do you, Anna? Any other girl might have packed her bags and gone only as far as the corner, but not you. You board the *Hindenburg*."

Anna opened her mouth to make a hot retort, then looked up and saw that his eyes were smiling down at her.

"I'm not any other girl," she said.

The smile in Erik's eyes got a little warmer. "I can see that you are not. I recognized that the moment I first saw you."

8/22

Look for these historical romance titles
from Archway Paperbacks.

Hindenburg, 1937 by Cameron Dokey
San Francisco Earthquake, 1906 by Kathleen Duey
(Coming soon!)

HINDENBURG
1937

Cameron Dokey

AN ARCHWAY PAPERBACK
Published by POCKET BOOKS
New York London Toronto Sydney Tokyo Singapore

AN ARCHWAY PAPERBACK *Original*

An Archway Paperback published by
POCKET BOOKS, a division of Simon & Schuster Inc.
1230 Avenue of the Americas, New York, NY 10020

ISBN: 0-671-03601-7

First Archway Paperback printing July 1999

10 9 8 7 6 5 4 3 2 1

AN ARCHWAY PAPERBACK and colophon are registered trademarks of Simon & Schuster Inc.

Cover art by Cliff Nielsen

Printed in the U.S.A.

IL 7+

For Jahnna and Malcolm, who passed
my name along.
For Fran and Lisa, who hung in there.
And for Hubert.

HINDENBURG
1937

Frankfurt, Germany, late April 1937

He was dying and there was nothing she could do.

Anna Becker sat at her grandfather's bedside, her icy hands clasped in her lap. She could feel her palms sweating where she pressed them tightly together. Knew that, if she unknotted her cramped fingers and dried her hands on the front of her skirt, she'd have done so a thousand times already, leaving the fabric rumpled and damp.

Anna's legs ached from the long hours of sitting in one position. Her neck and shoulders felt as brittle as eggshells, as if the slightest movement would cause them to snap.

She had a sudden vision of her head tumbling from her body like something from a children's bedtime story, while the rest of her body stayed in the chair, perfectly motionless.

Kurt would hate that, she thought. It wouldn't be what proper German young ladies did.

The unbidden thought of her older brother sent a hot spear of panic shooting across Anna's chest. She unclasped her hands and pressed cold fingers against the base of her throat, desperately trying to force the panic back.

Naturally, Kurt had been sent for when their grandfather fell ill, but he hadn't arrived yet. He had a long way to travel, all the way from Berlin. He'd been sent there several months ago, shortly after his eighteenth birthday, when his time in the Hitler Youth had ended and his military service began. Anna could still remember how thrilled he'd been.

"Berlin is where the important decisions regarding the future of our country are being made," he'd told her. And he wanted to be as close as possible to the great men who were making them.

At first Anna had missed her brother. Their grandfather's house in Frankfurt, never full to begin with, had felt even emptier without Kurt in it. But lately she'd come to dread Kurt's infrequent visits.

Every time he came home, Kurt seemed more and more different, less and less like the brother Anna remembered. It was as if his time in Berlin was turning him into a stranger. A stranger full of plans for her. Plans of which Anna wanted no part.

A sharp handful of rain spattered against her grandfather's bedroom window, startling Anna out of her reverie. She started, then squirmed in her chair, as if the seat with its plump cushion had suddenly grown rock-hard.

It's because I'm thinking about Kurt, she realized.

Just the thought of her older brother was enough to make Anna uncomfortable. The distance between them grew with each of his visits, and Anna had no idea how to bring him close again.

Even worse, she was no longer sure if being close to Kurt was what she really wanted. It seemed they disagreed about everything these days.

With fingers that trembled ever so slightly, Anna rubbed her hands against her skirt again.

"I do not understand you, Anna," Kurt had said impatiently on his most recent visit. As usual, they'd been quarreling about the way Anna spent her weekends. Kurt thought Anna should be part of the Hitler Youth, as he had been.

But Anna didn't want to spend her weekends dressed in a uniform, tramping around the countryside, pretending camaraderie with girls for whom she felt nothing. She wanted to spend them as she always had, at home with her grandfather, poring through the volumes in his library.

Even the name of the young women's unit, the Bund Deutscher Maedel, League of German Maidens, filled Anna with misgivings. She didn't want to be part of a league of young women, all taught to think the same things.

She wanted to be acknowledged for what she was: an individual, with her own thoughts and feelings.

She'd tried to say as much to Kurt, but he refused to listen. He disapproved of Anna's independent thinking, a trait for which he blamed their grandfather.

"Can you not see that the life you are leading is selfish?" he'd all but shouted. "That, by living in this way, you are neglecting your duty to the fatherland?

"If Grandfather truly loved you, he would not keep you here with him, filling your mind with dangerous ideas, allowing you to read books that he knows are not sanctioned. He would send you out into the world to do your duty and prepare you for your true destiny."

Anna had bitten her tongue to keep from shouting back, defying her older brother. But she was beginning to learn that the ideas she treasured most were the ones Kurt agreed with least. And so she hadn't told him what she was really thinking.

No one, not even her beloved grandfather, would plan her future for her. Anna herself would decide her true destiny.

A second gust of wind rattled the windows, a gust so strong it howled down the chimney. Anna's stomach tightened at the sound.

How that used to frighten me as a child, she recalled. *And it was always Kurt who came to comfort me, telling me stories of what we would be when we grew up.*

But her brother's visits brought her comfort no longer. Now Kurt told her stories of the future that were nothing less than horrifying.

Anna would be married, he said, to a man of her

brother's choosing. A man who was willing to overlook the fact that Anna's hair was too dark—not the
pale spun gold of corn silk but the deep amber of
honey, that her eyes were too pale, not the deep blue
of an alpine lake but the soft blue of a morning sky
in summer. A man who was willing to overlook the
fact that Anna's figure was small and slight, far from
ideal for childbearing.

It might be difficult to find such a man, particularly since Anna's behavior was so unsatisfactory. But
Kurt was confident he could do it. After all, he was
a rising star in the German army. His behavior was
above reproach.

And once she was married, Anna's must be also.
For the rest of her life she must be perfectly obedient
to her husband. She must do his will, never question
his authority. She must bear his children and raise
them to believe in the glory of the fatherland.

Just thinking about it made Anna shiver uncontrollably.

Please, she thought, as she stared down at her
grandfather's still, pale face, at his shallow breathing,
which barely stirred the coverlet. *Please stay alive.
Please don't die and leave me, Opa.* If her grandfather
died, Anna would have no one left but Kurt. No one
to help her stop her brother's plans for her.

"Anna! Why are you sitting here in the dark?"

At the sound of a voice from the doorway, Anna
jumped, then dropped her head into her hands. It
wasn't Kurt. Not yet.

"Ursula," she choked out. Her grandfather's housekeeper moved across the room with a rustle of the starched apron she always wore, her round face puckered with concern.

"There now, I didn't mean to startle you," she said, giving Anna's shoulder a gentle pat. "But you can't see how your grandfather's doing in the dark, and you must be cold. You've let the fire go out, and you've no sweater, as usual."

Anna almost smiled. Her grandfather's house was drafty, and his housekeeper was forever fretting because Anna never wore a sweater. Ursula's fussing was usually guaranteed to make Anna smile, but today she couldn't quite get the corners of her lips to curve upward. "I'm sorry, Ursula."

The truth was, she'd been so lost in her own fear that she hadn't noticed the progression of the hours making the room grow cold and dark around her. She'd thought the darkness was all in her own thoughts.

"There now," the housekeeper said again. She left Anna's side to move around the room briskly, stirring up the fire, drawing the curtains against the raw and rainy April evening, switching on a wall sconce. Slowly the colors of Anton Becker's room came back into view. The deep brown of the polished wood walls, the burgundy of the satin coverlet.

Anna watched, feeling comforted in spite of herself by the housekeeper's simple everyday actions. But then, Ursula almost always had that effect. She had been a presence in Anna's life for as long as Anna could remember.

It was Ursula who'd told Anna stories about her parents, dead almost before Anna could remember them. "Your parents loved each other so much, they couldn't bear to be parted. Not even by death," she had said.

When Anna's father was killed testing the new airplane he was designing, her mother had simply lost the will to live. Even her small children could not make her hold on to life. One month after her husband's accident Ilse Becker too was dead. Six-year-old Anna and eight-year-old Kurt had lived with their grandfather, their only surviving relative, ever since.

"Come downstairs and eat something, Miss Anna," Ursula said now, from her position on the far side of the bed. "You've been up here all day. You won't help your grandfather if you wear yourself out. You must pace yourself. You heard what the doctor said today."

"Yes, I heard him," Anna answered.

She'd heard him say her grandfather's heart, never strong, was giving out that day. As if it had suddenly taken on a burden too great for it to carry, a shock too great for it to bear.

But what that shock had been, not even Anna knew. Her grandfather would take that secret with him to his grave.

With another rustle of her apron, Ursula reached

over and switched on Anton Becker's bedside lamp. Anna winced at the sudden glare.

In the glow of the electric light, her grandfather's face looked even worse than it had that morning. Then his skin had been flushed bright red, as if he'd run a long race. Now it had paled to the sickly gray of fireplace ash.

Anna felt the panic rising, searing the back of her throat. "I can't leave him, Ursula," she said. "Besides, I'm not hungry."

The housekeeper's sympathetic eyes met hers across the coverlet. "There's been no change?" she asked.

Anna shook her head.

No change since the telegram had come that morning after breakfast, bringing to a screaming halt all their whispered confidences. Anna and her grandfather had been in the library, congratulating each other on the success of their plans.

"We will have an adventure, Anna," Anton Becker had declared, his blue eyes sparkling as he smacked his fist into the palm of his hand. "One not even your oh-so-proper brother can find fault with. Even he cannot argue against our making a journey on such a glorious symbol of the fatherland."

"The *Hindenburg*." Anna had whispered the name like an incantation.

After months of planning, Anna and her grandfather were going to travel on the great rigid airship's first voyage of 1937. On May 3, less than two weeks away, they would fly all the way to America.

"Well, now," Anton Becker had continued, rising from his favorite chair by the fire. "That's enough idle chatter for this morning. I have some correspondence to take care of, and you must have some packing to do."

"Grandfather," Anna protested, laughing. They both knew that she'd been packed for days. Ursula had protested that Anna's clothing would be wrinkled beyond recognition. Anna had said she didn't care. She was going on an adventure, not to a fashion show.

"Your pardon, Herr Becker." With a quick knock on the library door, Ursula had entered. In one hand she'd carried a silver tray with a piece of paper in the very center. "A telegram has just arrived for you."

"Thank you, Ursula," Anton Becker had answered.

"Who's it from?" Anna had eagerly asked.

Ursula had clicked her tongue on her way out of the room, but Anna's grandfather had chuckled indulgently and murmured, "Patience, Anna."

But by then his eyes were already on the message, and what he saw made his face turn sheet-white, then a harsh and fiery red. He took two stumbling steps to the fireplace and dropped the paper into the flames. He paused a moment, leaning against the mantel, and watched as the telegram burned to ashes.

Only then did he turn to Anna, but by then it was

too late. His hands were at his chest, his eyes bulging from their sockets as he struggled for breath.

"Anna," he'd said. Just once. Just that. Nothing more than her name. It was the last thing he'd said. The last thing he might ever say.

"You know that's not a good sign, that lack of change," the housekeeper said quietly.

Anna came back to the present with a brutal snap. Her beloved grandfather was dying before her eyes, and she could only watch, helpless. Her throat burned so that she could hardly force the words out.

"Yes, Ursula, I know that. But I will not leave him. Not until—"

"There now," Ursula said again.

Suddenly Anna could sit still no longer. Moving stiffly, she forced herself up from the chair. If she sat and did nothing for another instant, she'd begin to weep. Or worse, she'd begin to scream.

I can't afford to lose control, she thought. She couldn't give way to her fear and grief. Not now. Not yet. Not as long as there was the slightest chance her grandfather might still need her.

"Go stand by the fire and warm yourself," Ursula said, noting Anna's actions approvingly. She stepped away from the bed. "I'll fetch your sweater, then send you up a nice bowl of hot soup. Try to eat something, Miss Anna. You must be ready for whatever comes."

Whatever comes, Anna thought, as she listened to

the housekeeper's footsteps move off down the hall. *Whatever comes, I must be ready.*

Even if what came was the end of the only life she knew. Even if what came was death.

Anna shivered and was grateful for the sound of Ursula's returning footsteps. She reached for her sweater, but Ursula was too quick for her. She stepped in, took the sweater, and wrapped it around Anna's shoulders. For one moment Anna felt the housekeeper's arms around her. For just one moment she felt warm and safe.

Then Ursula released her and turned to go, closing the bedroom door softly behind her. Anna turned to face the fire, thrusting her arms into the sleeves of her sweater. In spite of the fire's heat, she shivered again, because she was almost certain she knew what was coming: if her grandfather died, Anna was in for the fight of her life. The fight *for* her life. And without Anton Becker there would be no one to fight beside her. She would have to do battle all alone.

"Anna."

Anna whirled at the whisper of sound from the bed. Her grandfather's eyes glittered in the firelight. He was awake at last.

"Anna," he said again, his hands moving restlessly across the coverlet.

"Opa!" Anna cried, moving swiftly to the bed to lean over him.

At the sound of her childhood nickname for him,

her grandfather smiled. But there was still no color in his face. His skin looked pale and stretched. It was plain that just keeping his eyes open was taking all his strength.

"Anna," her grandfather gasped again. "Anna, you must promise me—" He broke off, fighting for breath.

"Of course, Opa," Anna said soothingly. She laid her hand over his and felt her heart stumble in her chest. Her grandfather's fingers were even colder than hers. "I will promise whatever you want. Only rest now. You must gain your strength back."

Her grandfather's head moved back and forth on the pillow in restless refusal. "No time. There is no time, Anna. You know that. Use your head. You must—"

He reached out toward the nightstand, hooking one trembling finger into the pull for the top drawer. Gently, trying not to see the way her own hands trembled, Anna moved her grandfather's finger aside, pulled the drawer all the way out, and set it on the bed.

"What is it?" she asked. "Tell me what you want, Opa. I will get it."

But her grandfather's fingers were already scrabbling among his papers. Before Anna could prevent him, he struggled to raise himself up on one elbow, the better to see into the drawer.

"Wait, Opa," she cried in alarm. "Let me do it. Let me help you."

Anton Becker fell back against his pillows, something clutched tightly in his right hand.

"Anna, promise me," he whispered again.

Anna could feel the panic rising like a wave within her. *Anything*, she thought. *Anything*. "I promise, Opa," she said urgently. "Only, please, now you must rest."

Without warning, Anton Becker began to gasp, his left hand clawing at his chest. He pulled in a shuddering breath. His mouth worked, then stayed open. Before Anna could so much as move to summon help, he exhaled one long, slow breath.

Then he lay still, the fingers of his right hand still tightly closed around the paper he'd pulled from the nightstand drawer, his eyes still staring straight up at Anna.

It was over; her beloved grandfather was dead.

Anna sank to her knees beside the bed, her face pressed against the coverlet. Her grandfather had been the most important part of her life for as long as she could remember. What would she do now that he was dead?

"Promise me," he had whispered, trying to communicate his dying wish. With all her heart, Anna wished to grant it. But how could she? She didn't know what her grandfather had meant.

If only I'd been faster, she thought. *If only—*
She lifted her head.

"Anything, Opa," Anna whispered, as she stared

at him. "I will do anything for you. If only you will come back and tell me what you want."

Slowly, watching her hands as if they belonged to another person, Anna straightened the bedclothes, smoothed the hair back from her grandfather's face. In a moment, she knew, she must summon the rest of the household.

I don't feel anything, she thought. *That can't be right, can it?*

Carefully she rose to her feet and removed the crumpled paper from her grandfather's grip.

Pain rushed in then, filling every single cell in Anna's body. She felt something now. Something she wasn't sure she could bear, because she knew now what her grandfather wanted. She understood his final wish, the thing he'd wanted so much that he died trying to make her promise.

"Miss Anna Becker," the paper said. "May 3, 1937."

It was her ticket to travel on the *Hindenburg.*

2

"No!" Kurt Becker said forcefully, pounding his fist on the mantel for extra emphasis. "I do not know how you can even contemplate such a thing, Anna. It is absolutely out of the question!"

It was a week after their grandfather's funeral. A week that had seen the month of April turn to May. A week that had seen the end of Anna's old life and the beginning of her new one. A week that had seen the end of everything.

Her brother had taken charge from the moment of his arrival. He'd made funeral arrangements, called a meeting of the household staff, met with the family lawyers. He'd handled everyone and everything.

The only one he hadn't spoken to was Anna.

She'd been excluded from every meeting, every

decision, left to spend hours alone in her room. But even there Anna was always aware of her brother's presence. Kurt looked like some fierce bird of prey, the buttons on his uniform gleaming. Anna never knew what he would swoop down on next.

He'd had the library stripped the day after their grandfather's funeral.

Gone was the collection of books Anton Becker had spent a lifetime collecting, the basis of the ideas he'd shared so joyously with Anna, burned on an enormous pyre in the backyard. Kurt had even had the shelves removed and burned, as if to show that there would be no going back to the way things had been.

Not now. Not ever.

Once the library had been stripped of its offending ideas, Kurt had spent virtually all his time there. He'd claimed their grandfather's massive oak desk for his own, conducted all his business from it.

Finally he'd sent for Anna, but by then she had had hours on her own, days in which to realize what her brother was doing. Kurt was trying to impress her with the strength of his will, to show her that it would be useless to stand against him. But those long, silent hours alone in her room had also shown Anna that standing against Kurt was exactly what she had to do if she was ever to have a life of her own, and she knew that she could afford to let absolutely nothing stop her.

"But surely you can see that I *must* do this, Kurt,"

she said now, striving to keep her tone one of even reason. "Surely you can see that I must honor Opa's dying wish."

Kurt snorted. "I can see no such thing. I refuse to believe our grandfather wished for you to travel on the *Hindenburg* without him. That sounds more like one of your harebrained schemes."

Anna could feel her face begin to flush. She bit down hard on the inside of her cheek. She could not afford to lose her temper. The stakes were too high.

Why did I think that I could do this? Convince him that I'm right. Why didn't I just sneak off and be done with it?

But Anna knew the answer, even as she framed the question. *Because even now I can't believe he's a total stranger. Surely the brother I loved so much must be hidden somewhere inside this man.*

If he was, Anna hadn't seen him. How on earth was she going to get out of this impossible situation?

"Use your head, Anna."

It was the thing her grandfather had always encouraged her to do, the thing that only he had told her. And if ever Anna needed to use her head, the time was now. Somehow she had to find her brother's weakness and exploit it.

The trouble was, from where Anna was sitting, Kurt looked almost perfect. He was tall and broad-shouldered. His eyes were deep blue. His hair was the same color as Anna's, though—the deep gold of honey. It was the only way in which he differed from the ideal of the fatherland.

Can I play on that? Anna wondered. *On the importance of keeping up appearances?*

"I am only thinking of the family, Kurt," she ventured. "I am thinking of my duty. I would hate to have others say we did not do what is right."

"I am pleased to hear it," Kurt said shortly. "But no right-thinking person would expect you to make such a trip on your own, Anna. Our grandfather is dead, and I am the head of the household now. I am the one to whom you have a duty."

Bright pain shot through Anna. Pain she'd been doing her best to control all week. She lost her temper in a rush. "You're not sorry Opa's dead, are you?" she lashed out before she could stop herself. "You have what you want now—control over everything."

For a split second anger flashed across Kurt's face, along with something that looked like pain. Then both expressions were gone, leaving only determination in their place.

"You think you are so clever, Anna," Kurt said, his voice quiet and controlled, as if to highlight the differences between them. He would not be goaded as she had been. "You think you know so much, but you do not understand anything."

"I understand that you will not honor our grandfather's dying wish," Anna shot back, "that you will not do *your* duty."

"I have a duty greater than the one I owe our grandfather," Kurt answered in a tone like ice. "My duty is to my country, to my fatherland. And I have a duty toward you, Anna, even though you may not wish it. It is my duty to see that you behave appropriately.

"Did you really believe I would let you travel on the *Hindenburg* alone?" Kurt continued, his voice filled with exasperation. "A girl of sixteen traveling unaccompanied would draw the worst kind of attention."

"The worst kind of attention to *you*, you mean."

Two bright spots of color flamed in Kurt's cheeks. "Oh very well," he said passionately. "Since you are determined to quarrel, yes, that is also what I mean! I've worked hard to achieve my successes. I will not let you take them from me, Anna."

And what will you take from me, Kurt? Anna thought. But she had her temper back under control now, and so she said nothing. Instead she watched as her brother left his position in front of the mantel and knelt to take her hands in his. Only a supreme act of will kept her from pulling them away.

"Anna," Kurt said softly. "Please, you must listen. Things are not the same as when our grandfather was young. We are building a newer, stronger Germany, a land where all of us must do our part. That is all I am doing and all I want you to do."

"And what about what I want?" Anna asked, unable to help herself. "Do you care nothing for that?"

For a split second, her brother looked genuinely surprised. "But surely you must want what is best for Germany."

How can it be best for me not to think for myself? Anna wondered. *Not to be myself?*

But once again she said nothing. An idea was forming in the back of her mind, a notion she couldn't quite grasp.

Her grandfather's words echoed in her mind: *"Use your head, Anna."*

"What is it you want me to do, Kurt?" she asked.

Kurt's face cleared, as if the fact that she had finally asked the question meant that he had won and that she had given in. His hold on her hand tightened.

"I want you to come back with me to Berlin."

No! Anna's mind screamed.

Her hands jerked back out of Kurt's grasp before she could control them. This was the thing she'd been the most afraid of, the thing that had haunted her dreams—the thought of losing not only her grandfather but her home as well. She would lose everything.

"But surely I could not stay with you," she faltered. "You have no home of your own. You live in a barracks."

Kurt got to his feet. "That is true," he admitted shortly. He settled into their grandfather's favorite chair, his presence there only underlining the fact that Anton Becker was gone. Anna could hardly bear to look at her brother.

"But I have been giving much thought to this," Kurt continued. "I've been in touch with my commanding officer about you, Anna. Colonel Holst has a daughter just your age. He has been anxious to find a suitable companion for her."

So that's it, Anna thought. Her future was to be worse than her worst nightmare. She'd already lost her grandfather. Now, she would lose her home as well, and her brother would put her into the hands of strangers.

"The colonel has offered to take you into his household. Being seen with Fraulein Holst will be a great advantage for you, Anna. Under the colonel's protection, you will meet all the right people. We will soon find you a suitable husband. Your future will be secure."

And yours, too, Anna thought. *Most important, yours too.* Her hands clenched, convulsively, her fingernails digging into her palms.

Anton Becker's voice rang in her memory: "Use your head, Anna."

Oh, Opa! she thought desperately. *How I wish you were here to help me.*

But he had already helped her, she realized, as she looked at her older brother, staring at her so confidently. The one thing Kurt did not want was for Anna to think for herself.

Yet that is exactly what I must do. And I must do

21

more than just think for myself. I must act for myself, too. And I must never, ever let my brother know what I am doing.

You are wrong about me, Kurt, Anna thought. *I do understand things. I see your weakness. And I know how to outsmart you.*

Slowly she willed her fingers to relax.

"But what of Ursula and the rest of the servants?" she asked, striving to make her tone deliberately subdued.

"Our grandfather provided for Ursula in his will," Kurt said, his tone dismissing the woman who'd cared for him almost his whole life. "The rest of the servants are young and will easily find other employment. The young men should be doing their duty in the army. The women should marry or work in a factory."

Well, that's that, Anna thought. *It's so simple for you. All of us in our proper place.* All cogs in the well-oiled machine that was a strong and powerful fatherland.

She lifted a hand to rub her forehead as if her head hurt. All of a sudden she realized it did.

"When do you wish to return to Berlin?"

"At the end of the week," Kurt answered. "I should be able to finish up my affairs here in Frankfurt by then."

"I see," Anna said. She forced herself to rise to her feet slowly. What she really wanted to do was to leap up and run from the room. Run as far away as her legs would carry her and never stop.

"With your permission I will go and begin packing."

"Anna." Kurt rose swiftly. In two steps he was beside her. Anna looked up into her older brother's face. Kurt's brow was puckered slightly.

Just for an instant Anna was sure she saw uncertainty, maybe even regret, in his eyes. He looked like the brother she remembered from her childhood, the one she'd trusted. The one she'd loved. Then the expression vanished, as if he'd drawn a curtain across it. *You really are a stranger*, Anna realized. *Not because you must be, but because you choose to be.*

"I am pleased to see you are taking this so well," Kurt said, with an attempt at a smile. "I thought you would protest more vigorously."

And I thought you were smarter, brother. Anna never would have been able to fool the old Kurt. But fooling this new Kurt was easy. He had stopped using his head, his eyes, his heart. He saw only what he wished to see.

For the last time, Anna did not speak her thoughts. There were so many things she was not supposed to think, so many thoughts it wasn't safe to say out loud.

"I know you are only doing what you feel is best, Kurt," she said softly.

"I *am* doing what is best for you, Anna," Kurt said. Then he gave her a dazzling smile. Relief swept through Anna so suddenly she felt dizzy. She'd done it. She had convinced her brother that she'd given up. He believed that he had won.

"You'll like Berlin," Kurt assured her. "You'll see."

"I'm sure I will, once I get used to it," Anna answered. She swayed a little on her feet. "May I go up to my room now? I am a little tired."

"Of course," Kurt said at once. He released her arm. Anna walked across the library. Just as she grasped the doorknob, Kurt called after her. "It really *is* for the best, you know, Anna."

Anna felt the spot between her shoulder blades begin to itch. She was certain that her brother was looking at her, but she didn't turn around. She knew that if she looked back now she might lose her courage. If that happened, she'd be lost for good.

"I'm sure we'll both do what we think is best, Kurt," she answered quietly. She pulled open the library door, stepped through, then softly closed it behind her. Then she leaned against it for a moment, savoring the quiet.

Anna closed her eyes and felt the house, so familiar, all around her. She held her breath and heard the steady ticking of the grandfather clock farther down the hall.

I am going to leave the only home I can remember, she thought. *I am going to leave all of this behind. But not in the way Kurt thinks.*

The Hindenburg *sails tomorrow night. I am going to be on it, no matter what it takes.*

And I am never coming home.

I can do this. I must!

Late the following afternoon Anna stood in the lobby of the Hotel Frankfurter Hof, waiting to clear the checkpoints that would enable her to board the bus that would take her to the airfield and the *Hindenburg*.

Anna told herself she ought to feel safe. She'd completed the first part of her plan, the first step away from the life her brother had mapped out for her. She'd reached the Frankfurter Hof while Kurt was on his way back to Berlin.

"May I take a walk this morning, Kurt?" Anna had asked at breakfast that morning. Hands clenched into fists beneath the table, she'd taken care to keep her voice low and soft. "I want to say good-bye to

Frankfurt. It may be a long while before I see this city again."

Across the table, Kurt had actually smiled at her. "But of course you may do so, Anna. It will be good for you to say farewell. I'm sorry that I can't accompany you."

But Anna wasn't sorry. Her morning walk was just an excuse, a means to accomplish two important things: she'd arranged for a taxi to take her to the Frankfurter Hof late that afternoon. And she'd arranged to send her brother a telegram, scheduling it to arrive later that morning.

There would be plenty of time between her walk and the telegram's arrival, enough time so that Kurt would never connect the two events. Besides, he wouldn't expect anything so bold from Anna. He wouldn't expect her to think or act for herself.

Sending her brother a telegram seemed only fitting to Anna. A telegram had taken her grandfather from her. Now one would take Kurt also, not by his death but by Anna's carefully constructed lie.

The message she'd sent had said, "Colonel Holst dangerously ill. Important you return Berlin at once."

Upon its arrival, Kurt had responded exactly as Anna had hoped. He'd caught the first train back to Berlin. Anna had known exactly which one it would be. She'd taken care to check the railway timetables.

Kurt had promised to send for her as soon as he could. But by the time he reached Berlin and discovered he'd been tricked, Anna would be safely aboard the *Hindenburg* and on her way to America.

But I'm not there yet, she thought. In fact, her goal of reaching the airship seemed farther away than ever. All around the lobby, Anna could see people having their tickets validated, their passports checked, and their luggage examined. At any of these points, Anna could be stopped and turned back. She could feel the palm that clutched her suitcase grow sweaty at just the thought.

Don't panic. Use your head, Anna.

The trouble was, her head told her that Kurt had been right about one thing: by traveling alone she could very well attract unwanted attention. The longer she stayed on her own, the greater the chance that someone could notice her.

That made this stage of her plan even more dangerous than getting out of the house, because it meant that she must put her trust in a total stranger.

Somewhere in this sea of people, she must find someone willing to pose as her traveling companion.

Well, I can't do it on the outside looking in. Pulling in a deep breath, Anna moved farther into the bustling lobby.

Instantly the noise increased. It seemed to Anna that every single person around her was talking. She didn't know which way to turn. Which station should she go to first?

"No! Mama! I won't let him take my car away!"

Anna staggered back as a small body hurtled into

her. She looked down to see a young boy clutching a metal toy car tightly in one fist.

"Franz!" said a woman's voice. "Come back here this instant. My apologies, fraulein," she went on, as she reached Anna.

"It is nothing," Anna answered. "Can I help?"

"This car is mine," the boy answered, holding the toy up. "My present from Papa. It isn't right for that man to take it." He turned and pointed. Anna saw a young man in a customs uniform bearing down upon them. She felt her knees begin to shake.

"Hush, now, Franz," the boy's mother said. Swiftly she knelt beside him. With deft fingers, she pried the car loose from his tight grasp. "You must not fuss so. The official is only doing his duty."

"But the car is mine," the boy protested again.

As Anna watched, the mother rose and handed the toy car to the customs official. A blaze of gold insignia decorated the breast of his uniform. His boots were so highly polished that Anna could all but see herself in them. Everything about him radiated authority.

But to Anna's surprise the official knelt beside the boy and ran the metal toy across the lobby's red plush carpet. Tiny sparks shot out the back.

"That is why I must take this, do you see?" he asked the youngster. "Nothing that can make a fire is allowed on board the airship."

"But—" the boy said.

The official's expression hardened. "No more protests, now," he commanded brusquely. He rose to his feet. "Your mama is right. It is my duty to take this away, just as it is yours not to question why I must do so. Don't you wish to do your duty to the fatherland?"

The mother gave a startled gasp. Her face had turned sheet-white. "But of course he does," she said in a voice that trembled ever so slightly. "It's just that he's so young—"

Her voice broke off as the custom official's eyes swept over her. "No child is too young to be made to understand his duty," he answered coldly. "Now I will check the rest of your luggage over here." With a brisk gesture of his hand, he motioned to a nearby table. The mother seized the young boy's hand and dragged him off.

In spite of what she'd just witnessed, for one brief moment, Anna considered following. Appearing to be part of a family was the best protection she could wish.

But something about the way the mother had been so swift to turn her son's beloved toy over to the official held her back. Surely she'd be just as swift to turn Anna over. With her, Anna would have no protection.

Frowning, she turned away, once more surveying the lobby. Across the room, a line of people waited to have their tickets validated and their passports checked.

Safety in numbers, Anna thought. Grasping her

suitcase a bit more firmly, she moved to join the line, using her progress across the lobby to observe her fellow passengers more closely.

Near the head of the line several people knelt with their backs to Anna beside what looked to be a dog kennel. Anna couldn't tell which of them owned the dog. Toward the end of the line stood an elderly couple, the wife with her arm tucked securely into her husband's. His head was bent low, toward hers.

Perhaps that couple, Anna thought. She could appear to be traveling with her grandparents. Anna saw no other likely prospects. Most of the line seemed to be made up of men her father's age or older.

Anna stepped to the back of the line and set her suitcase down, keeping her body still, though her thoughts were in furious motion. The older couple definitely seemed like her best choice, but how should she approach them?

"Clumsy oaf!" a man's voice suddenly exclaimed. "Why don't you watch what you're doing?"

The reply of the man so addressed was drowned out by a quickly subdued burst of laughter. Quickly Anna shifted her position, stepping out of line a little so she could see what was causing the commotion.

The men at the dog kennel were standing now. Near the head of the line Anna could see a dark head bobbing up and down. *What on earth?* she thought. Then she realized what the young man was doing.

He was hopping.

With one hand he clutched his foot. With the other he gestured to the carrying case belonging to the man behind him. All the while he continued hopping up and down, up and down.

In a flash of inspiration, Anna thought she understood: the second man had dropped his carrying case on the first man's foot.

Anna felt a grin spread across her face, even as she sympathized with the injured party. His dark hair flopped across his forehead as he continued to bounce up and down. Even across the room Anna could see his expression. He looked absolutely furious.

Not just hopping, but hopping mad.

She felt a sudden burst of excitement.

Unlike most of the men around him, this man was young, only several years older than Anna. At the moment he was literally off-balance. He might not wish to endure any further embarrassment or attract any more amused attention.

And he was traveling alone, Anna realized. While many passengers had turned to see what was going on, no one had taken his part or offered to help him.

Anna made a split-second decision, propelling herself forward before she had time to think the situation over. She kept her eyes straight ahead, zeroing in on the dark-haired stranger.

"Oh, there you are!" she cried gaily as she approached him. "For heaven's sake, what mischief have you gotten yourself into this time? Can't I leave you alone for even a second?"

The dark head swiveled toward her. The foot he'd been holding dropped to the floor and stayed there. "I beg your pardon?"

Summoning every ounce of courage she possessed, Anna took one final step forward and laid a hand on the young man's arm. The wool of his dark suit jacket was scratchy beneath her fingers. Anna squeezed. Hard. As if by touch alone she could make him understand what it was that she so desperately needed.

She glanced up into his face, preparing to make one more teasing remark to win him to her side, but she felt her throat close up.

She'd never seen anything like his eyes.

They were green. But a shade of green Anna had never seen in a pair of eyes before. Deep and glistening, like the holly Ursula brought into the house at Christmastime. The pupils were brilliant and dark, surrounded by a thin band of gold.

Like a ring around the moon, Anna thought. The kind one would see in a clear night sky right before the storm clouds swept in.

Gypsy eyes, Anna thought. Dangerous, glorious, alluring eyes. Staring up into them, she forgot all the clever phrases she'd hoped would persuade him to help her. She even forgot why she needed help in the first place.

All she could do was stare upward, completely unaware of the yearning in her own eyes. *Don't ask questions*, they said. *Just say yes. Just help me.*

She saw his nostrils flare as he pulled in a quick breath. Saw those ink-black pupils widen. The circle of gold expanded with them, making his eyes burn with sudden light. Then he smiled, and Anna felt her own breath stop.

He was going to help her.

"So here you are," the young man said lightly. He closed his fingers over hers and Anna felt her whole body warming. Her heartbeat pounded in her ears. She could feel the blood rushing just beneath the surface of her skin.

Where did such heat come from? she wondered.

She'd been cold with fear ever since she left the house, but all this stranger had to do was touch her fingers to drive the cold away.

"Apparently you *can't* leave me alone, even for a moment," the stranger continued. "I need you . . . as you see."

He cocked one dark eyebrow at her, the expression in his forest-green eyes becoming slightly challenging. He flexed his fingers against hers, as if to remind her it was her turn to carry on their game, whatever it was.

Abruptly Anna realized she was still staring up at him, her mouth open like a hooked fish.

"Are you all right?" she managed, her voice coming out in a squeak.

The young man's smile got a little wider. Then

his gaze flicked up, to rest on something just behind Anna. Belatedly she remembered the man with the carrying case.

What on earth is happening to me? I've got to pull myself together.

"Of course I'm all right," the young man answered, though Anna couldn't tell if he was addressing her or the man behind them.

"Such a small valise couldn't really hurt me so easily. I became annoyed, that is all. Such an incident is so unnecessary. I apologize for my outburst. I hope there are no hard feelings."

His tone was still light, but Anna felt the warmth inside her vanish as quickly as it had come. She fought against a sudden need to shiver. There was something running like a swift current in his voice. Something hard and dark and dangerous.

"Anna?" said a voice behind her.

Anna jolted, as if she'd heard an expected sound in the quiet dark. Her fingers clenched around the stranger's arm.

It can't be, she thought. *It mustn't.*

Her heart began to beat in double time, so hard that Anna could see the front of her coat quiver with it. She locked her knees to keep from swaying on her feet.

She was vaguely aware that the young man beside her had shifted his attention away from the man who stood behind them. Now he was focused on Anna herself.

When he saw the expression on her face, he made a low sound in the back of his throat and wrapped his free arm around her to support her. Anna could feel the strength of it even through her coat. She was grateful for the extra support.

I'm going to need it, she thought. *All of it. Everything this stranger has to give and more.*

Because she knew that voice. She knew who stood behind her. Knew who'd dropped the carrying case on her rescuer's foot.

I'd know that voice anywhere in the world, she thought. And wished she didn't hate herself quite so much for it.

Slowly, still within the circle of the dark-haired man's arm, Anna turned to face the man who, against all odds, stood behind them. She saw his blue eyes, fathomless as the ocean, range across her face, then come to rest upon her own.

"Anna," he said slowly. "Anna Becker. It is you."

"Hello, Karl," Anna said.

Karl Mueller, the man she'd once been certain she would love forever.

4

She wanted to hurt him.

It was all Anna could think of as she stood there staring up at him, her body hot and cold by turns until she didn't know if she would burn or freeze. She knew what she wanted, though, with her whole soul.

She wanted to hurt Karl Mueller.

She wanted to pay him back, to hurt him as much as he'd hurt her, to make him suffer as she had suffered.

But more than anything else, Anna wanted to look into Karl Mueller's eyes and see that he knew she felt absolutely nothing for him.

Unfortunately, she wasn't doing a very good job of showing him that.

Damn you, Karl Mueller!

Anna felt her sudden rush of anguished feelings give way to a flood of bright red fury. She didn't want to care about Karl Mueller. Had done her best not to care about him.

I worked so hard to get over you, she thought. So hard, she'd mistaken her effort for accomplishment. But now she realized the truth. She was a long way from being over Karl Mueller. How could she get over him when she remembered every single word they had ever spoken?

"I told you we would find her here," her grandfather had said one bright Saturday morning last August. Anyone else might have been outside, but Anna had been in the library as usual, her face buried in a book.

"My dear, I'd like you to meet the grandson of my oldest friend. This is Karl Mueller. He's going to take you for a walk in the park and put some color into your cheeks. Karl, this is my granddaughter, Anna. Come on, girl, get your nose out of that book."

"Give her a minute, Anton," Karl had said. "At least let her finish the chapter."

Her grandfather had given a bark of laughter. "Two of a kind," he'd said. "I should have known it."

"Anton," Karl had bantered back, "if I didn't know you better I'd say you were trying your hand at matchmaking."

"And what's wrong with that I'd like to know?" her grandfather had shot back.

Finally, in self-defense if for no other reason, Anna had looked up—and known that nothing was ever going to be the same from that moment onward. Just one instant. That was all it had taken for her life to change—for her to fall in love with Karl Mueller.

His eyes were exactly the right shade of blue, like deep, still water. His hair, an impossible shade of blond so fine and pale it all but glistened when the sun shone on it. His body was lean and taut. Something about Karl always reminded Anna of a sleek cat, ready to spring.

Their passion had sprung up quick and hot, then run like summer wildfire. All through the brisk days of autumn it had kept them warm. But in the winter it had turned to ashes. Anna could still remember their last day together.

They'd gone to the park, the same one they'd strolled in that very first morning. Karl had taken her ice-skating. He had whirled her around and around until she was dizzy and breathless, then held her so close that there were no longer any space between them. Held her until they weren't two people; they were one. Anna had been certain they would stay that way forever.

"Anna, I have to go away," he'd murmured.

And in yet another instant Anna had felt her life change once again. Karl would give no reason, no explanation. He would only repeat that he had no choice. The pain of that moment still had the power to steal her breath.

"You may not walk me home as if this were any other day!" she'd said. "Do you think I'll behave like a good little girl and make this easy for you if you behave like a perfect gentleman?

"If you have to go, just do it, Karl. Go now, so I can watch you walk away. I want you to feel my eyes on your back with every step you take. I want you to know that's the last thing I'll ever see of you and that I won't ever forget."

Without another word, he'd turned and left her. Anna had stood in the park until her feet were numb with cold, her breath a thick cloud around her in the frigid air.

Just one instant, she thought now. That was all it had taken for her to give her heart away. The same amount of time it had taken for Karl Mueller to break it.

But things would be different this time, she vowed. This time Anna would be the one to walk away.

"What a surprise to see you here, Karl," she said, at long last breaking her silence. Anna was pleased to hear her voice come out light and steady, with no hint of her inner turmoil. "Are you traveling or just seeing someone off?"

"Traveling," Karl answered shortly, his eyes shifting to the dark-haired man behind her. Anna became aware of him again suddenly. Aware of the still, alert way he held his body so close to her own.

"And you?" Karl asked. But his eyes were still on the young man. Abruptly Anna felt as if she'd taken a plunge into cold, deep water.

Something about the way Karl looked at the other man suggested to Anna that the two of them knew each other.

But Anna didn't know the man she was with, this stranger she'd selected to help her, who now stood so close behind her. She didn't know anything about him, not even his name, but she could not afford to let Karl know that.

Once she would have sworn that Karl would do anything rather than hurt her. Now she had direct proof to the contrary.

"It's been so long since I last saw you, Karl," she said before the man behind her could speak. "I did not expect to see you again."

As if her cool words reminded him of his own actions, Karl started. His eyes jerked back to her face. Then, just as quickly, he recovered his composure. He gave away nothing of what he was feeling.

"I did not expect to see *you* here, Anna," he answered.

Anna bit back a retort of anger and pain. She was not as good as Karl at concealing her feelings, but she knew that this was hardly the time to be outspoken. Bitter words just now could put her entire plan in jeopardy.

The trouble was, her throat ached from wanting to hurl angry, hurtful words at him. *So soon after my grandfather's death, you mean? So soon after the funeral you never bothered to attend?*

But then she had not expected her grandfather's death to prompt Karl Mueller to return to her. He'd abandoned Anton Becker just as surely as he'd abandoned Anna. His defection was one of the few topics Anna had refused to discuss with her grandfather, with whom she usually shared everything.

"I am fulfilling a duty to my grandfather," she said coldly, and watched in surprise as Karl's face flushed with sudden color.

"Anna, I—"

"Anna," a low voice in her ear interrupted. "I'm sorry to intrude. But is that fellow over there trying to attract your attention?"

The dark-haired man behind her pointed, resting one arm atop her shoulder as he did so. It was the gesture of someone with whom Anna felt at ease. Someone who had her permission to touch her casually.

Suddenly Anna could feel his other arm, still warm against her back. And she saw Karl's eyes narrow.

I see how things are now, she thought. *You do not want me, but you do not want anyone else to have me. Well, I do not have to play this game according to your rules.*

"I don't think so," she answered. It was the elderly man she'd noticed earlier, the one who'd gazed so tenderly at his wife. Now he gestured to Anna, pointing to something near his feet. As she realized what it was, Anna relaxed against the stranger with a low laugh. "He's pointing to my suitcase," she answered. "In all the excitement of seeing you hopping up and down, I'm afraid I walked away and left it."

"Scatterbrain," the dark-haired young man murmured warmly. "Now I see what happens when I let *you* out of *my* sight."

Oh, perfect, Anna thought. And watched as Karl's expression hardened. In the next moment she felt the breath catch in her throat as the arm across her back became as hard as a bar of iron.

The older man's waving had caught the attention of one of the customs officials responsible for the luggage. He strode over, exchanged a few quick sentences, then picked the suitcase up and made his way purposefully toward Anna.

"Is this your suitcase, fraulein?" he asked as he approached.

Anna could feel her heart begin to thunder, but she did her best to answer calmly. "Yes, it is. I didn't mean to leave it. It's just that I got into line before I—"

Anna was startled into silence when the officer shifted his attention to Karl, clicking his heels together smartly. "Your pardon," he said. "I did not see you there, Herr Mueller. This young lady is your travel companion?"

There was a pause the length of a heartbeat.

"*Nein,*" Karl answered softly.

Anna's heartbeat became a steady roar in her ears. Karl had done no more than speak the truth, but it felt as if once more he had denied her.

The official set her suitcase down and turned toward her. Anna felt his eyes examine her from head to foot, then shift to the young man who stood behind her.

"The young lady travels with you?" he inquired.

Anna felt the arm at her back tighten until she was sure her bones would crack. But the dark-haired man's voice was perfectly smooth when he responded, "I am a friend of the family."

Clever answer, Anna thought, even through her terror. Her companion hadn't really answered the question, but the officer didn't seem to notice.

"Passport," he demanded abruptly. With fumbling fingers, Anna dug her passport from her coat pocket. The officer took it from her and thumbed it open. "Ticket?"

Anna produced her ticket from her other pocket. The officer studied it, lips pursed. Without a word he picked up her suitcase, spun on his heel, and walked away. Anna's knees began to tremble uncontrollably. Had it not been for the strength of the arm at her back, she was sure she would have fallen.

It is over, she thought. *Somehow my brother has discovered my deception. The official is going to contact him. In a moment Kurt will come to take me home. I will never be free again.*

Soft as eiderdown, she felt the dark-haired young man's breath beside her ear.

"Courage, Anna. Never give up, even when things look darkest."

Anna took a deep breath to steady herself as the official strode back toward them.

"I have validated your ticket, Fraulein Becker," he said, handing it back to her, "as everything seems to be in order. Your suitcase will be searched. I suggest you do not let it out of your sight a second time. I regret it cannot be returned to you now. But you will find it waiting in your cabin when you board the *Hindenburg*. Your passport will be kept for the duration of the flight."

"Oh, but—" Anna gasped.

"All passports are being retained in this manner," the official interrupted her. "They will be returned when the airship reaches America. The bus is now ready to transport passengers to the airfield. If you will allow me to escort you . . ." his voice trailed off.

It sounded like a question, but Anna knew that it wasn't. She felt the arm at her back fall away. Her fingers like ice, she took the elbow the official offered. As they stepped away, Anna refused to look at Karl, who had denied her. Instead, she glanced back into those forest-green eyes.

"Save me a seat, Anna," her rescuer said.

Unbelievably, Anna felt her lips curve upward. "Never give up," he'd counseled her, "even when things seem darkest." And he'd been right. If she'd given up, she would have given herself away. Then all would have been lost.

I can do this, she thought once more, as she had when she first entered the lobby. *I* will *do it, for myself and for Opa*. She would let nothing stand in her way—not her own fear, not the unexpected appearance of Karl Mueller.

She would board the *Hindenburg* and never look back. All the way to America.

5

An hour later Anna stood on the airfield, the collar of her coat turned up against a light rain, staring up at the great silver bulk that was the *Hindenburg*.

Already outside its giant hangar, tethered by its nose cone to its movable mast, the swastikas on its tail fins illuminated by an array of searchlights, the airship looked like a great whale about to be released to swim through the heavens. Never in her life had Anna seen anything so big.

As big as what I'm trying to accomplish.

She watched as a gust of wind shifted the airship, causing the ground crewmen to shout and cling to their mooring lines. After a few moments of strenuous pulling, they maneuvered the ship back into position.

Even the Hindenburg *is eager to be off,* Anna thought.

She had seen the airship before, of course. Just last year, when it had made a triumphal flight across all of Germany. It had sailed over every major city in the country, dropping leaflets urging support for the policies of Adolf Hitler.

Almost everyone in the city had turned out to see the great ship flying overhead, along with its sister ship the *Graf* zeppelin. But Anna had never seen it on the ground. This close up, it was absolutely enormous. As long as three football fields, she'd heard one of the American passengers proclaim excitedly.

A short way back from the nose, just where the slope of the ship began to level out into its long, cigar-shaped body, the control car rested on the ground, supported by its center landing wheel. It looked like a tiny life raft clinging to the enormous silver body of the airship.

How, Anna wondered, *could something so small control something so big?*

A short distance behind the control car, above the ground and actually inside the *Hindenburg*'s hull, were the passenger accommodations. Anna could see lights shining down from a bank of windows. The sight was warm and welcoming.

"Look!" a woman's voice called. "They are lowering the gangways."

Heart kicking, Anna watched two narrow stairways drop down from the center of the passenger area.

All I have to do is to walk up one of them, she thought, *and sail away to freedom.*

As if the lowering of the gangways had been a cue, the band that stood in the airfield's visitor section begin to play *"Deutschland, Deutschland, über Alles."* Beside the band, a group of Hitler Youth in their swastika-emblazoned uniforms cheered and shouted.

Anna looked away. The young men reminded her far too much of Kurt.

"We can board now. Are you ready, Anna?" a quiet voice said. She turned to find the dark-haired stranger once again beside her.

Anna still didn't know his name, a fact that bothered her. But she'd had no opportunity to ask it on the bus ride from the Frankfurter Hof. By accident or design, Anna didn't know which, Karl had been seated right behind them. She could hardly ask the stranger who he was under those circumstances.

As a result, she'd hardly said a thing all the way to the airfield. She was grateful that the young man hadn't pressed her to break her silence. Anna felt so tied up in knots that she was afraid to say anything at all for fear of betraying her inner confusion.

The sooner I'm on board, the better, she thought now.

"Yes, let us go," she answered, doing her best to give her companion a brave smile. "I am ready."

His hand lightly supporting her elbow, the young man steered her across the field toward the gangways along with the other passengers.

The young boy Anna had seen earlier tugged

against his mother's restraining hand. A girl about her own age walked silently between her parents. A group of men who all looked alike to Anna laughed among themselves.

"I assure you it is true," she heard one of them say. "This great behemoth provides such a smooth ride that you can stand your pen on end and it won't fall over the entire voyage."

And then suddenly Anna felt the rain stop as the body of the airship loomed above her. Half a dozen more steps, and she'd be at the bottom of the starboard gangway. Behind her she heard the band begin a rousing march.

I am going to do this, Opa, she thought. *I am going to make you proud of me.*

She withdrew her elbow from the young man's grip, suddenly determined to board the airship without assistance.

I am on my own now, she thought. *It's time I started acting like it.*

Placing her hand on the gangway banister, Anna set her foot on the first step and began to climb. A moment later she forgot everything else as she felt the great airship surround her. Even though she was so eager to be on board she could have sprinted, Anna forced herself to move slowly.

Take it easy, she told herself. *One step at a time.*

But it took her almost no time at all to reach the lowest level, B deck, even moving slowly. She could not see much of it from the stairs, but she caught a glimpse of a narrow hallway carpeted in soft red. Promising herself she'd explore this level later, she swung to her left and continued upward.

The second flight of stairs, leading to A deck and the main passenger accommodations, was much like the first, once again ending in soft reddish carpet. By the time she reached the top, Anna's heart was pounding as hard as if she'd run a race.

I'm aboard the Hindenburg. *I've done it.*

In the next moment she was surprised to find herself face to face with her dark-haired companion. He'd come up the opposite staircase. His green eyes danced as if he'd perpetrated some great mischief.

"How did you get over there?" Anna exclaimed. "I thought you were behind me!"

His grin matched the mischief in his eyes. "I thought you might like the first face you saw on board to be a friendly one," he answered.

Heedless of the fact that there were other passengers behind them both, he stepped out onto the A deck landing and bowed low, clicking his heels and extending one bent arm. Anna took it, laughing, all her earlier fears forgotten.

Together they turned to see the elderly couple Anna had noticed at the Frankfurter Hof, speaking to a pleasant-faced woman dressed in a white uniform and a close-fitting white cap. In one arm she cradled a clipboard.

She gestured, and the couple moved off in the direction she had pointed. With a rush of emotion,

Anna saw the husband reach out to take his wife's hand just before they vanished from sight.

How wonderful, she thought, *to be loved like that*.

A moment later she felt her companion's fingers tangle with her own. Startled, she looked up, and once more found his face alight, daring her to say he'd gone too far this time. But the truth was, Anna didn't have the faintest idea what to say. Her companion's actions were a constant surprise to her.

He was so different from Karl Mueller and so different from her rigid, unyielding brother. They had surprised her, too, but their surprises had been painful ones.

Looking up into his laughing face, Anna felt a surge of optimism. Surely the fact that the first person she'd chosen to trust in her new life could surprise and delight her—challenge her, even—was a good omen.

"We're blocking traffic," he murmured now, giving her hand a quick tug to pull her forward.

"That didn't seem to bother you before," Anna murmured back, and was rewarded with a chuckle.

"Good evening," the woman in white said pleasantly as they stopped in front of her. "Please allow me to make you welcome. I am your stewardess, Frau Emilie Imhof. If I may make your voyage more comfortable, you have only to ask."

Anna could hardly speak over the excited pounding of her heart. "Thank you," she managed to get out. "Can you direct me to my cabin?"

"What is your name?" the stewardess asked.

"Anna Becker."

"Ah, yes, Fraulein Becker," Frau Imhof said, consulting her clipboard. "Your cabin is down this corridor." She gestured toward the port side of the airship. "The second door on the right. You are on the dining room side of the ship, fraulein. In the evenings, you will find it is much quieter."

"Thank you," Anna said.

"And you, sir?" the stewardess asked.

"I will see the young lady settled first," Anna's companion answered.

"Very good," Frau Imhof said.

With a second tug on her hand, Anna's companion led her down the corridor the stewardess had indicated. Like the one she'd glimpsed on B deck, this hallway was narrow—so narrow they could barely stand side by side. Cabins lined both sides of the corridor.

"Here we are," Anna's companion said. "Fraulein Anna Becker, second on the right." With his free hand, he reached out to slide Anna's cabin door open.

Anna cast a quick glance inside. Her immediate impression was of plain practicality. A bunkbed stood against one wall. An aluminum ladder provided access to the upper bunk. The carpet was a soft pearl gray. Anna's suitcase stood in the very center of it.

The cabin was far too small for her to invite her companion in, even if she'd been tempted to do so.

"I think I'd like my hand back now," she said.

Her companion gave a low laugh. "And I think you're a teller of tall tales, Miss Anna Becker. You don't know quite what to do with me, but no matter. I don't know quite what to do with you, either. I guess that makes this a voyage of discovery, doesn't it?" Still holding her hand, he raised it, stopping just short of his lips.

Anna felt her whole body begin to tingle. What would those smiling lips feel like, pressed against her skin?

"Down here, Mama!"

The voice of the small boy she'd seen at the Frankfurter Hof made Anna start. With an exhalation that sent his warm breath flowing over her knuckles, Anna's companion released her.

"Until we meet again, Miss Anna Becker," he said. Then, neatly avoiding the forward rush of the young boy, he moved off down the hallway. Anna stepped into her cabin and slid the door closed behind her.

He's right, she admitted to herself. *I don't know what to do with him. I guess this will be an adventure in more ways than one.*

The only thing she could be sure of was that her dark-haired companion, whoever he was, would continue to surprise her.

6

"Oh, my goodness, my dear! I do beg your pardon!"

Anna was back out in the corridor. She was too excited to stay in her cabin. Besides, there was no reason she had to explore it right that moment. There would be plenty of time to do that after the *Hindenburg*'s departure.

But no sooner did Anna slide open her door and step out than she all but collided with the passenger whose cabin was directly opposite.

"Please, don't apologize," Anna said to the older woman who stood before her. Then she blinked in surprise. She had shed her coat in her cabin, revealing the white blouse with short puff sleeves and dark knife-pleated skirt she wore beneath. The lines of Anna's clothing were smooth and simple.

But the woman in front of her wore an outfit the likes of which Anna had never seen before. To her startled eyes, the older woman seemed to be made entirely of fluttering ruffles, an impression that was reinforced when she began to flutter her hands as well.

"Oh, my goodness!" she exclaimed again. "We should be taking off at any minute. No matter how many times I do this, I never get used to it. Isn't it exciting?"

Anna opened her mouth to speak, but the other woman spoke again before she managed to utter a single syllable. She stepped forward, linking one arm with Anna's. "Is this your first voyage?" she asked, as she propelled Anna ahead of her down the corridor. Deciding it was safer to say nothing, Anna simply nodded.

"It is good to start young," the woman said approvingly. They reached the end of the corridor. "Best not to wait until you are my age to look for adventure."

Anna couldn't help it: her mouth dropped open. It was so exactly the opposite of everything her brother had ever said but so close to what she herself wanted.

At the expression on Anna's face, the older woman gave a peal of silvery laughter.

"I'm s-sorry," Anna stammered. "It's just—"

"I understand," the woman interrupted. "It's not a popular opinion these days, I know. But when you're my age, you don't have to worry so much about what other people think."

At that moment Anna stopped thinking entirely.

As they'd been speaking, the older woman had piloted Anna past the stairs, then turned and doubled back on the far side, along the hallway that ran from one side of the airship to the other.

Now they stepped through the doorway. To Anna's right was the dining room. She had a swift vision of dazzling white table linens, sparkling crystal and silver. But it was the view immediately in front of her that had rendered her speechless.

Here were the windows she'd noticed before. From the ground, Anna hadn't thought much about them. But now that she was actually on board, she realized just how large they truly were. Standing in front of them once the ship was in flight, Anna was sure she could see the whole world open up before her.

"Oh, my goodness," she said, finding her voice at last. "This *is* exciting."

The older woman laughed again. "It gets better," she promised. "I'll show you. Come, let's go to the promenade."

She guided Anna over to the windows. A group of men moved over for them. Now Anna could see the airfield below them, the searchlights glowing. In their bright light, she could see the ground crew, still clinging to the mooring ropes.

"They'll release them on the captain's signal," the

older woman said. She let go of Anna's arm to lean against the promenade railing. "Then they'll help push us off, and the captain will release the ballast water."

"Ballast water," Anna repeated. It was a term she'd never heard before.

"We must lift off as level as we can," explained the man standing nearest to her. "Carrying water adds extra weight. Releasing it helps to keep the airship in alignment as we rise."

"Thank you," Anna said. "That is my first lesson in airship flying."

The man smiled. "My pleasure, fraulein."

"Gracious, my dear," said the woman in the ruffles. "Keep that up and you'll be the belle of the voyage."

The man turned back to his companions, laughing.

"But how rude I'm being," the older woman went on. "I've all but dragged you out here without an introduction. Please allow me to introduce myself. I am Frau Grete Friedrickson."

Anna put her hand into the one Frau Friedrickson extended. "I am Fraulein Anna Becker," she responded. "It is a pleasure to make your acquaintance."

Anna felt the older woman's fingers tighten around hers, the strength of the grip surprising.

"Never refuse an offer to shake hands, Anna,"

Opa had always told her. "A handshake can reveal a person's true personality."

Now Anna was surprised by what Frau Friedrickson's handshake revealed about her. This was a woman who knew her own mind, not a woman whose head, like her clothing, was filled with ruffles. Intrigued by the difference between the woman's appearance and her handshake, Anna squeezed back.

"So, Fraulein Anna Becker," the older woman said, as she released Anna's hand and turned back to stare out the promenade windows. Following her friend's lead, Anna could see that the group of Hitler Youth had moved much closer to the airship.

"What do you think of this great monster so far?"

"I think it is wonderful," Anna said impulsively.

More wonderful than even she had dreamed of. More than that, it was the escape vehicle that would take her from her old life to her new one.

Anna had no idea how she would survive on her own once she reached America. She only knew she was determined to try. Naturally, she confided none of this to Frau Friedrickson.

"I am happy to have a cabin on this side of the ship," she said instead, determined to keep the conversation going. "The stewardess said it would be quieter."

"The lounge is on the other side," Frau Friedrickson explained. "Although it is supposed to close at eleven o'clock, if you retire early, it can be noisy.

"I am happy to be on this side of this ship, as

58

well" the woman went on. "I had originally been told that no more cabins were available on this side but when I boarded . . ." She shrugged. "Oh, well, perhaps someone decided not to travel at the very last moment."

Her voice trailed off as she caught a glimpse of Anna's face. "What is it, my dear? Have I said something to distress you?"

"No," Anna protested. "It's just . . ." She gave up, decided to tell the truth. There was no way around it. She hadn't been quick enough to hide her feelings. "My grandfather was to have traveled with me," she admitted softly.

Anna felt Frau Friedrickson's eyes on her. Her eyes were like her handshake, shrewd and strong.

"I see," she murmured in a voice that plainly said she did not but was too polite to say so.

"He died recently," Anna continued haltingly. "I know you must think it is too soon for me to travel," she continued in a rush. "But my grandfather wanted me to make this trip. On his deathbed he pleaded with me."

"Then I will say nothing of the sort," Frau Friedrickson said promptly. "If you honor your grandfather's deathbed wish by making this trip, you are doing what is right. But surely you cannot be thinking that I have his cabin, my dear. You must be traveling with some other member of your family."

Now I've done it, Anna thought. She hadn't meant

to confide so much, but there was something about Frau Friedrickson.

"No," Anna said, her voice barely above a whisper. "No one else accompanies me."

This time Frau Friedrickson's eyebrows winged up. But once more all she said was "I see."

Anna could feel panic, like an itch between her shoulder blades. She'd taken such pains to find a companion to board the airship with her. Now here she was, admitting she was traveling alone before the *Hindenburg* had even departed. And in the middle of the promenade, where anyone might overhear her.

I must be insane, she thought.

In the next moment she jumped as a shout echoed throughout the ship.

"*Schiff hoch!* Up ship!"

Now she could hear other orders being shouted as the mooring lines were released. Anna forgot her fear of discovery in her rising excitement. She was really going to do this.

"I'm going to fly!" she exclaimed.

Frau Friedrickson gave another peal of silvery laughter. "You are indeed, my dear," she said. "Watch now. I have a feeling about those ardent young Nazis below us."

Anna leaned forward to look downward. She heard another shouted order. As she watched, a group of ground crewmen surrounded the passenger area, giving it a mighty shove upward, then quickly moved back. The Hitler Youth crowded in to take their place, cheering and waving.

A few moments later, in the rapidly gathering twilight, Anna could just make out an enormous spray of water. A burst of laughter swept the promenade.

"I thought so," Frau Friedrickson said, chuckling. "That happened the last time, too, I'm afraid."

"What?" Anna asked. "What has happened?"

"The crew knows enough to get out of the way, but sometimes the spectators on the ground follow the airship a little too closely," Frau Friedrickson answered. "I'm afraid our Hitler Youth have just been baptized with the ballast water."

Anna joined in the general laughter, then cocked her head to one side as she heard a new sound. The great diesel engines of the *Hindenburg* had started up, then settled down to a deep thrum, like the purr of some enormous jungle animal.

For one split second as she looked down, Anna felt disoriented. Weren't the beams of the searchlights getting smaller? And she could no longer see the Hitler Youth just below them.

In the next instant, Anna realized the truth. The *Hindenburg* was rising so smoothly that she hadn't even felt a tremor. Anna heard the tone of the engines change, growing even deeper and realized that the great airship had begun to move forward.

She had done it. She was in the air and safe. And on her way to her new life in America.

Without warning, the enormity of what she was

doing—what she had done—hit Anna square in the stomach. She swayed and felt Frau Friedrickson reach out to steady her.

"There now," the older woman said, her tone an exact match for the one Ursula always used to comfort her. Anna blinked, startled to find she was battling back tears.

"Now that we're under way, the first order of business should be some dinner," Frau Friedrickson counseled. "You go have a quick rest while I see to it that we're seated at the same table."

She drew Anna away from the promenade windows. "Don't worry. I won't turn into an old pest. In fact, if you prefer it, I won't say a word during dinner. Though, naturally, I hope you don't prefer that. A young lady who embarks on such a journey all on her own must be very interesting to talk to, don't you think? And I'm no slouch in the conversation department."

"Frau Friedrickson," Anna managed, feeling completely bowled over.

The other woman's flow of words stopped. Her eyes looked into Anna's.

Brown, Anna thought. Not a deep, rich blue that could not be trusted.

"Yes, my dear?" Frau Friedrickson said.

"I—" Anna started.

"That's quite all right, my dear," the older woman interrupted. "I'm happy to do it. No need to thank me."

Anna gave a sputter of helpless laughter. The other woman's behavior was unusual, to say the least, but Anna had to admit that it was effective. Anna no longer felt the urge to burst into tears. In fact, she felt much better.

It's going to be all right, she thought.

And for the second time that day she knew that she'd been right to trust a total stranger.

"There is one thing you can do for me, my dear," Frau Friedrickson said, as she once again maneuvered Anna forward.

"What is it?" Anna asked, biting back a smile. She thought she was beginning to understand how Frau Friedrickson operated. Perhaps the ruffles were nothing more than a clever disguise.

"I don't know about you," Frau Friedrickson said, as they moved down the hallway to their cabins, "but I see nothing wrong with a little male companionship on our voyage. I hear there are some handsome young men aboard this ship. If I were you, my dear, I'd wear my prettiest dress to dinner."

7

"So you see," Frau Friedrickson said later that evening. She thrust her fork into an asparagus spear and bit off the top of it.

How can she do that? Anna wondered. *I'm so excited I can't eat a thing.*

But then, Frau Friedrickson wasn't changing her entire life, as Anna was. And this wasn't the older woman's first zeppelin voyage. For the rest of her life, Anna knew she would remember the moment she'd stepped back into the dining room after dressing for dinner.

Although "dinner" had turned out to be a cold buffet due to the late hour of the *Hindenburg*'s departure, the dining room was decked out as if for a formal occasion, and so were the passengers.

The stark white tablecloths accentuated the dark coats and pants of the men. The flowers that adorned each table harmonized with the colored evening dresses of the women. The soft, flowing fabrics reminded Anna of so many butterflies, flying and alighting.

Although she'd heard the dining room steward say the *Hindenburg* wasn't full, carrying just thirty-six, a little over half of the usual seventy-two passengers, the dining room still seemed full of color, motion, and sound to Anna.

A group of intimate tables for two ran the length of the railing that separated the dining room from the promenade. Longer tables for six or more stood on the promenade side of the railing.

On the opposite side of the dining room, stretching the length of its pale fabric wall, a series of colorful scenes depicting the *Graf* zeppelin's frequent flights to Rio de Janeiro added a bright touch to the room's otherwise austere elegance.

Everything about the public areas was designed to make the passengers feel pampered and comfortable. And to remind them that zeppelin travel was the experience of a lifetime.

Even the table service added to the overall effect. Anna's fine white porcelain plate was bordered in blue and gold and embellished with the zeppelin company's insignia.

On each plate, a white zeppelin floated across a blue globe. The image was so detailed that Anna could even see the parallels and meridians covering the globe like a tiny gridded blanket.

It's a good thing I admire my plate so much, Anna thought wryly, *as I haven't been able to eat a single thing I put on it.*

Frau Friedrickson swallowed the last of her asparagus.

"So you see," she said again. "My son-in-law decided it was the best way to get rid of me. Pack the old lady off on the *Hindenburg*, where she'll cause no trouble. Or at least no trouble to him."

"He didn't!" Anna protested.

Frau Friedrickson gave her tinkling laugh and toyed with one of her bracelets. Her evening attire was more subdued than her daytime outfit. There wasn't a ruffle in sight, but a series of silver bangles dangled along each wrist. Anna wasn't fooled by her friend's laughter, however. For once, Frau Friedrickson's eyes were not laughing.

"Oh, yes, my dear," the older woman answered. "I'm afraid he did. My daughter's husband is a creature of this great 'new Germany' we hear so much about. One who believes that women are suited only for childbearing.

"If he had his way, not one woman would be allowed to have a brain in her head. And I'm sorry to say he suits my daughter perfectly. She was so happy to see me go that she all but packed my bags."

Although she had spoken in a light, amusing tone,

Anna could see that her traveling companion was deeply upset.

We have more in common than you realize, Frau Friedrickson, she thought. *My family doesn't want or appreciate me, either, now that my grandfather is dead.*

She hesitated a moment, then decided to take the plunge. "My brother wished to send me to Berlin to live in the home of his commanding officer," she confided, "so that he could find me an acceptable husband."

At once, Frau Friedrickson's expression lightened. She made a tsking sound of disapproval. "Men can be such idiots, can't they? As if you weren't perfectly capable of choosing a husband for yourself."

Suddenly she brightened. "My dear," she said. "I think you've acquired another admirer. There's a green-eyed young man just behind you who's been watching our table all evening. I don't flatter myself that it's because of me. Turn around slowly, now. You don't want to call attention. Not the fat blond with the pimply face. The green-eyed one sitting right beside him."

"I'm not going to turn around at all," Anna protested, but she felt her pulse rate quicken.

All of a sudden she was glad she'd followed Frau Friedrickson's advice and worn her new dress for this first evening. At least she knew she looked her best, though she had to admit the dress was slightly daring. Made of pale blue silk exactly the same color as Anna's eyes, its halter top was cut low, the material soft and clinging. The waist was tight, the skirt, long and slightly flaring. It created just the impression Anna wanted. Chic. Sophisticated. A young woman would have to be very sure of herself to wear a dress like this.

It will be good for him to see me looking like this, she thought. *Good for him to see I have a friend in Frau Friedrickson.* She couldn't let him think she was alone and helpless.

"A green-eyed young man helped me board the airship," she said as neutrally as she could.

"Well, then," Frau Friedrickson said, "so you know him."

"Not well," Anna said. "In fact, I don't even know his name."

"I think all of that is about to change, my dear," Frau Friedrickson murmured. "Unless I'm very much mistaken, he's about to join us."

"Good evening, good evening," a hearty voice she'd never heard before said beside her.

Anna was so surprised, she jumped, jabbing her fork into a strawberry. Bright red juice squirted out onto her plate.

"For heaven's sake, Otto," a woman's voice chimed in. "Look what you've done. You didn't get any on that lovely dress, did you?"

"No," Anna answered. She looked up to find the older couple she'd noticed during boarding.

"I must apologize for my husband," the woman went on, though the tone of her voice was warm and affectionate. Their arms were linked, Anna noticed, as if they went everywhere joined together. "He did so want to meet everyone our first night out."

"Otto Ernst," the man said, thrusting one hand out first to Anna, then to Frau Friedrickson. Both shook it. "I am the oldest person on this voyage," he said proudly.

"And I am his younger wife, Else," the woman added, giving her husband a light dig in the ribs. "Somehow you keep forgetting to mention that, Otto."

Frau Ernst gave Anna a tiny wink.

"I don't forget," her husband blustered. "You just don't give me time to bring it up, Else. Uh-oh," Otto Ernst went on, leaning down as if to speak to Anna in confidence. "The time has come for us old goats to step aside, I think, and make room for the young stallions."

"For heaven's sake!" his wife exclaimed. "Mind your manners, Otto."

"I hope to see you again," Anna called as the couple moved off to the next table.

"Thank you, my dear. I'm sure we should both like that," Frau Ernst said over her shoulder.

A moment later Anna heard the sharp click of heels being smartly clapped together.

"A pleasant journey so far, is it not?" said the smooth voice she recognized instantly. "So many interesting passengers. May I have the honor to wish you good evening, ladies?"

"The honor is ours, I am sure," Frau Friedrickson answered, plainly determined to be on her best behavior. But Anna could see her shrewd eyes appraising this new arrival.

"Surely there is no need to stand on ceremony, since we will be travel companions for the next few days," she continued pleasantly. "I am Frau Grete Friedrickson."

She extended her hand. Anna watched as the dark-haired man took it, bowed over it, his lips just grazing the back of the older woman's knuckles.

"Erik Peterson at your service, Frau Friedrickson."

Frau Friedrickson's eyes were twinkling again as she let her hand drift back down to rest on the table.

"A pleasure, I am sure, Herr Peterson." She gestured across the table to Anna. "And this is my companion, Fraulein Anna Becker. Anna, Herr Erik Peterson."

"Delighted," Anna said. Erik turned toward her. Once more, Anna felt the full impact of those gypsy eyes on her.

He's going to have to kiss my hand now, she thought.

In slow motion she watched herself raise her hand, watched as Erik Peterson stooped to capture it. His lips brushed her knuckles, just the slightest touch, but one that sent every nerve in Anna's body jangling. He smiled as he released her hand, as if he knew exactly the effect he'd had on her: the one he wanted.

"I've already had the pleasure of making Fraulein Becker's acquaintance."

It isn't fair, Anna thought. *He ought to look more polished, more civilized, in his evening clothes, but somehow he doesn't.*

The stark contrast between his white shirt and black coat only made him look like a vagabond in a gentleman's stolen garments, rough-cut and dangerous.

"Have you, indeed?" Frau Friedrickson asked, when Anna didn't answer, having found she couldn't. "Perhaps you will join us for coffee, since we are now old acquaintances."

"I would like that very much," Erik Peterson answered. "That is, if Fraulein Becker agrees."

For one split second Anna thought she felt the brush of Frau Friedrickson's foot against her leg beneath the table. She couldn't tell if she'd imagined it or not, but it was enough to stir her into action.

"But of course," she said, just a little too loudly. She took a deep breath to slow the beating of her heart, and considered kicking herself. *Get ahold of yourself, Anna.*

"Please," she said, her voice sounding more normal. "But we will have to find a chair—"

"If you will permit?" a brisk voice interrupted her. Anna looked up to see the dining room steward standing over her. In one hand, he held a chair.

"Thank you," Anna said. "May we also have some coffee?"

"But of course, fraulein," the steward said. He seated Erik, then glided away, signaling a waiter.

"Is this your first passage on the *Hindenburg*, Herr Peterson?" Frau Friedrickson asked, as they waited for their coffee.

"By no means," Erik answered. He paused as a waiter appeared with a tray carrying a silver coffee-pot, cream, and sugar.

"Thank you," Frau Friedrickson murmured as the waiter deposited the items on their table. "Anna, will you pour?" At this signal that he was no longer needed, the waiter clicked his heels and departed.

"Of course." Anna poured three cups. Before she could ask what he wanted in his, Erik had already added cream to his coffee.

Anna watched, fascinated, as he stirred it in, his coffee spoon never once touching the sides of his delicate cup.

"Last year I made several crossings," he went on.

"You have business in America, then," Frau Friedrickson observed.

"Mmm," Erik answered as he took a sip of coffee.

Again Anna felt something brush against her leg beneath the table, though Frau Friedrickson's attention stayed on Erik Peterson. This time Anna knew she hadn't imagined it.

"The chief steward told us we're only about half full, this trip," Anna said, striving to make conversation. "That seems surprising, doesn't it?"

Erik shrugged. "Oh, I don't know," he answered

idly. "Perhaps the novelty has simply worn off. And last year, of course, we had the added attraction of the Olympics."

"Of course, the Olympics," Anna said. How could she have forgotten?

So much for making brilliant conversation, she thought. By now Erik Peterson's initial interest had no doubt evaporated and he'd written her off as a lost cause.

He probably thinks I'm a stupid schoolgirl in her older sister's borrowed dress, suffering from a first crush. Perhaps I should complete the impression and talk about the weather.

"Oh, look, there is Captain Pruss," Frau Friedrickson said, once again piping up to rescue Anna. "I always find it so reassuring when the captain joins the passengers, don't you? Such a civilized little ritual. And such a handsome young man with him, though not another officer, surely. He's not in uniform."

Anna turned her head to look down the promenade and found herself staring straight into the eyes of Karl Mueller. Even though he was still several tables away, Anna felt surprise tingle through her body. Karl's eyes had always had the power to startle her; they were such an impossible shade of blue.

At the moment Karl's blue eyes were harsh and brilliant, as if a thin sheet of ice covered them. Anna could almost see herself reflected in it, but she could read no hint of what Karl was feeling.

"He must be here in some official capacity," Frau Friedrickson prattled on, as if she hadn't noticed that all conversation at her table had ceased abruptly. "He's been at the captain's side all night. You would not have seen it, Anna, since your back is to that part of the room."

"Perhaps he is a cultural attaché of some sort," Erik Peterson suggested, setting his silver coffee spoon in his saucer with a sharp clink. "Though naturally," he went on in a lazy voice, "that could just be a civilized name for it."

With an effort, Anna jerked her attention away from Karl and brought it back to the man who sat at her table.

She remembered the moment in line when she'd had the impression that Karl and Erik knew each other, the strange current flowing between them that had told her the two were connected.

Was it true? she wondered. Did Erik know something about Karl? Something he was trying to tell her without really saying it?

"A civilized name for what?" she asked, her voice sounding sharper than she intended.

Erik took another sip of coffee, watching her over the rim of the cup. He waited until he had once again placed the cup in exactly the center of the saucer before he answered: "The term is useful; it can cover such a broad range of duties. Saying you are a cultural attaché might mean you do just about anything, might it not?"

Anna's breath faltered. She felt as if she were sinking slowly into a freezing river. She could almost feel the blood in her veins turning into solid ice.

She knew the thing Erik hadn't wanted to say aloud. The thing it could be dangerous, even fatal, to say.

Karl Mueller was a spy for the Nazis.

8

Anna's breath hitched in her chest. She put her hand to her head as a fit of dizziness swept over her.

I've got to get out of here, she thought. *Somewhere where Karl can't see me. Where I can't see him.*

Abruptly she pushed her chair away from the table.

"Please excuse me," she managed to get out. "I am feeling unwell. I think perhaps . . . a walk. I'm sorry. I'm so terribly sorry."

Then she turned and ran, heedless of Frau Friedrickson's concerned exclamation. Anna didn't know where she was going. All she knew was that she had to get out of the dining room, away from the ice-blue eyes of Karl Mueller—the eyes of the man she'd once loved with her whole heart, the man who had abandoned her. Had he done things even worse? Had she ever really known him?

I can't think this way, Anna thought. *I can't think about him.*

Choking back a strangled sob, Anna stumbled into the corridor that connected one side of the ship to the other. The pale fabric on the walls was a blur, the soft red carpet muffling her frantic footsteps as she dashed along it.

In the one corner of her mind that still functioned, Anna was grateful that most of the passengers were still at dinner. It meant she was unlikely to encounter anyone.

Not until Anna had almost reached the far side did she slow her pace, feel her nausea begin to abate. She managed one deep breath, the first she'd pulled into her aching lungs since she'd made the connection Erik had been wise enough not to speak aloud.

Karl Mueller is a spy for the Nazis.

Choking back a strangled sob, Anna dashed through the far doorway. Finally she breathed a sigh of relief. She was on the other side of the ship now, as far away from Karl as she could get. Though it didn't feel like far enough.

Karl Mueller is a spy for the Nazis.

It was almost too incredible to be true. But it made perfect sense to Anna.

Karl's sudden passionate interest in her. His equally sudden departure. Had her grandfather discovered the truth? Had he ordered Karl to leave and not come back?

Although Anton had rarely voiced his opinions aloud because of Kurt, Anna knew how her grandfather had felt about the Nazis. Unlike much of the rest of the population, he thought they were ruining the country.

"Yes, we are more prosperous now," he had said. "We have good things to eat. But look around you, Anna. Look for the neighbors you can no longer see. Too many have disappeared without a trace, without a warning. It is they who are paying the price of this Nazi prosperity."

Quickly Anna moved along the starboard promenade, past the lounge. She caught a quick glimpse of a group of men who looked alike to her, sitting around a table in animated conversation. A mural depicting the routes of the great explorers decorated the wall behind them. In the far corner of the lounge a small dapper man tinkled idly with the keys of a piano.

This side of the ship was a mirror image of the other. But instead of a single dining room, two rooms, the lounge and reading room, bordered the promenade.

Anna passed the deserted reading room and sank exhausted into a seat at the very end of the promenade, desperately trying to think back on the afternoon when her grandfather had tried to discuss Karl with her.

Opa had spoken of Karl only once after the younger man's abrupt departure. He'd brought the subject up during one of their quiet moments in the library. Anna had left the room to avoid discussing it. For the one and only time in her life, she'd refused to listen to her beloved grandfather.

If I had, would I have learned the truth? Was Opa trying to tell me the truth about Karl?

Anna put her head down into her hands, her thoughts whirling painfully. If Karl had kept this from her, had he ever told her the truth?

What if everything he told me was a lie? Even when he said he loved me.

"Anna."

Anna jerked her hands away from her face. The *Hindenburg*'s soft carpets had undone her. She hadn't heard Erik's approach.

"I'm sorry to intrude," he said in a low voice. "But Frau Friedrickson became concerned about you. Are you all right?"

Anna opened her mouth to reply, but no sound came out. She knew she could never explain; she didn't even know how to begin.

"I'm sorry," she said, as she had at the table, and felt hot tears prick at the back of her eyes.

With one fluid motion Erik reached out and eased her to her feet. "Anna, stop that, now. There's no need to apologize to me."

"I'm sorry," Anna said again. Erik made a soft sound, of what Anna couldn't tell, and put his arms

79

around her. He pulled her close. Anna felt the ice inside her melt as her blood began to race.

I'm so warm when I'm with him, she thought. *How can that be possible?* She'd never known the kind of heat she felt with Erik's arms around her.

She could hear his heart beating just beneath her cheek. The sound was vivid, vital. She could feel her own heart begin to beat to the same rhythm and knew the worst was over. She was back in control of her emotions now. She wasn't going to cry all over him. And she wasn't going to think anymore about Karl Mueller.

"Thank you," she said, easing back a little. Erik's arms tightened for a fraction of an instant before he let her go. "I'm much better now."

"That's quite an accomplishment," Erik said, his tone light, "considering you were practically perfect to begin with."

Anna smiled at the outrageous compliment. But she had to admit it made her feel much better.

"You have rescued me twice today," she said, working to match his tone. "I have not yet thanked you for the first time."

"No thanks are needed. I was happy to assist you," Erik responded. He offered his arm. Together he and Anna strolled back down the promenade. In just the brief time Anna had been there, the promenade had grown more crowded. Dinner must be over.

The pianist in the lounge was playing a popular show tune. Several voices began to sing along. Their noise would cover anything she might say, Anna decided. She took a deep breath.

"Nevertheless, I would like to thank you . . . and to offer an explanation."

Erik stopped walking. "You do not need to do this, Anna."

She wished it were true. Knew it was not.

"Yes, I do," she insisted. "The man we were discussing just now, the one with Captain Pruss. I know him. His name is Karl Mueller. He is—he *was*—a friend of my family."

"A close friend," Erik stated quietly.

Anna felt the color rise in her cheeks. But she refused to back down. She had started this, and she would finish it. "Yes, a close friend," she admitted softly.

"So you knew about him," Erik said.

"No." Anna's denial came swiftly. "I didn't know until this evening. That is why I left the dining room so abruptly. I simply could not take in the truth."

Erik began to walk once more. "I understand," he said.

But you don't, Anna thought. *You can't possibly.*

"If Karl is . . . what you suggest," she went on haltingly, "then I may have put you in danger by asking you to help me. I never would have done so if I'd known what he was. I'm sure Karl wouldn't approve of what I'm doing. He might even try to stop me."

"And what are you doing, Fraulein Anna Becker?"

Erik asked, his green eyes on her face, the gold deep within them shimmering.

Changing my life, Anna thought. *Making it what I want.*

"I'm running away from home," she answered.

Erik gave a low whistle. "You don't do things by halves, do you, Anna? Any other girl might have packed her bags and gone only as far as the corner, but not you. You board the *Hindenburg*."

Anna opened her mouth to make a hot retort, then looked up and saw that his eyes were smiling down at her.

"I'm not any other girl," she said.

The smile in Erik's eyes got a little warmer. "I can see that you are not. I recognized that the moment I first saw you. It's why I agreed to help, I think. Don't worry, your secret is safe with me, Anna. I'll guard it as safely as I would my own."

Anna tried to think of a clever reply—tried and failed.

"Thank you," she said softly.

They reached the end of the promenade. The song in the lounge ended to a spontaneous burst of applause. As it died down, Anna cocked her head. A sound she hadn't noticed before seemed to fill the air around her.

"What's that?" she asked.

Erik imitated her action. "I think it's raining," he answered.

Silently he maneuvered Anna out of the prome-

nade and into the deserted cross-corridor, as if he
understood her unspoken desire for privacy. "So,"
he continued, "you must have someone to go to in
America."

"No," Anna answered steadily. Now that she had
started, there was no reason now not to tell him all
of it. "I have no one. But I had to go. It was my
only choice."

Erik was silent for a moment. "I understand what
it means to make difficult choices, Anna. But perhaps
I can offer you one that's not quite so painful. Will
you honor me with your company during the rest of
the trip? I meant what I said. I would like this to be
a voyage of discovery for us."

Once more Anna felt her heartbeat quicken. This
time she knew it was with pleasure. It would be perfect to spend the rest of the voyage with Erik, she
thought. He was a perfect antidote for her confused
feelings for Karl.

And if the situation bothered Karl, so much the
better.

"I should be delighted," she answered.

Erik's face lit up in a smile, and Anna felt her
already speeding heart rate falter. His eyes were dazzling when he smiled, emeralds set in beaten gold.

"I'm so glad to hear that, Anna. And now I must
say good night—unless you would like me to escort
you to your cabin?"

"No, thank you," Anna said. "That will not be
necessary."

Erik reached out to capture one of her hands. Then, to Anna's surprise, he turned it over and ran one finger lightly over her palm, lingering on her wrist, at exactly the spot where her pulse beat. Then he lifted her hand and replaced his finger with his lips.

Anna felt her pulse leap, knew he felt the change in rhythm. His mouth lingered till Anna's heartbeat became a roar in her ears. She was sure she would feel the imprint of his lips long after all other sensation had faded.

"Good night and . . . sweet dreams, Anna."

There's not much doubt about that, Anna thought as she watched him gracefully turn back toward the lounge. Erik had definitely given her something to dream about.

And it would be something far more pleasant than what he'd revealed about Karl.

9

The next morning Anna woke early as was her habit. She lay in bed for a moment, listening for the sound of the rain. But she could no longer hear it. The deep, steady thrum of the engines was all she could detect.

This would be her first full day on the *Hindenburg*, she realized. She threw back the covers and climbed out of bed, filled with anticipation for the first time in days.

The first time in weeks, she amended as she pulled a matching robe over her white silk nightgown. *For the first time since Opa's death, I feel free, because I've done it. I've escaped.*

Anna still didn't know how she would live once the *Hindenburg* reached America. But she was sure she could find a way.

In the meantime she had something exciting to look forward to: her blossoming romance with Erik Peterson. She could feel the sleeve of her robe brushing softly against her wrist at exactly the place where Erik's mouth had lingered. Anna swore she could still feel the heat of his lips there.

What a perfect end to all my brother's careful plans, she thought, as she began to get ready for the day. *Frau Friedrickson is right. I am capable of choosing for myself. And Erik Peterson might be just what I want.*

She crossed to the wall opposite the bunk and eased open the pull-down sink. She turned the left-hand knob and hot water flowed from the tap. Anna splashed it over her face, then toweled her face dry and pushed the sink back up into its resting place. Then she simply couldn't help herself; she pulled it down again.

While she was getting ready for bed the night before, she'd had to stop herself from behaving like a small child, folding the sink up and down, up and down, just because she was so intrigued with the way it functioned.

Because the cabin was so small, there was no place for Anna to hang her clothes. They would have to remain in her suitcase for the short duration of her voyage, a fact that had Anna smiling as she recalled Ursula's point of view on the subject.

But Anna didn't mind the cramped quarters. The cabin on the *Hindenburg* was hers and hers alone. Everything about it absolutely delighted her.

The upper bunk folded up so that she wouldn't bang her head against it. During the day, the lower bunk could be made up into a couch. To one side of the head of the bunk, a writing desk could be dropped down in much the same manner as the sink.

Before she'd climbed into the bunk the night before, Anna had laid another of her new dresses out on the cabin's folding stool. She shrugged out of her nightclothes and began to dress.

For today she'd chosen a day dress of lightweight red wool. Its wide shoulders and black cinch belt accented her tiny figure.

Kurt would hate this dress, Anna thought. *He'd say the color would attract too much attention to me. That it was too bold for a proper German young lady*. But it wasn't too bold, not for Anna. For her, it was absolutely perfect. She sat on the stool to give her hair a quick brushing, then completed her outfit by fastening on a pair of black suede heels. Tiny silver buckles winked at the end of the ankle straps.

Feeling excited and confident, Anna folded the stool up and went to her cabin door.

Perhaps she would confide her late night meeting with Erik to Frau Friedrickson over breakfast, though she doubted the older woman would be up yet. Over lunch, then, Anna decided, as she slid the door open.

Karl Mueller was standing on the other side.

Anna took a quick step back. It was all she could

do not to yelp in surprise. Her blood pounded in her ears, but somehow she managed not to cry out.

Karl stood with one arm raised, fist lightly clenched, as if he'd been about to rap on her door. At the sight of her, he dropped his arm abruptly.

"Anna," he said, "I thought you might be up early. I was just coming to see you."

Oh, were you? Anna thought, and hardened her racing heart. "What do you want, Karl? I can't imagine we have much to say to each other."

And I don't want to see you.

Karl's face darkened, the only clue that Anna's dart had gone home. "Actually," he said, "I have a great deal to say to you, but not here in the corridor. The captain has arranged for us to have a moment of privacy in the smoking room."

For one wild second Anna considered refusing to meet with him. Then the reality of what she'd learned last night struck her in the gut like a hard blow. She could not say no to Karl. It could be dangerous to reject him.

"I haven't had my breakfast yet," she said, then hated herself for sounding like a spoiled and pampered brat.

"This will only take a moment," Karl assured her, as he reached out to take her arm. At the last moment Anna pulled away.

"I am not a child, you know, Karl. I know where the smoking room is. I think I can walk there all on my own."

"Just as you wish," Karl said. He stepped back and gestured for her to precede him along the corridor.

But Anna could see the way his jaw had clenched and was unable to resist one final shot: "And if I said I did not wish to go at all?"

"Then I would be forced to say you didn't have a choice, Anna."

Anna felt a shiver ripple down her spine. Without another word she stepped out into the corridor. When they reached the landing, Karl moved ahead of her, leading the way down the stairs to B deck. Neither of them spoke a word.

Anna tried to stay calm as they traversed the narrow corridor that led past the passenger toilets, then on to the bar and the smoking room. She tried not to be startled by the sight of a uniformed crew member, standing at the far end of the hall. And she tried not to fear the worst when she heard Karl instruct the crewman to let no one disturb them under any circumstances. He nodded once, his eyes straight ahead. Not once did he look at Anna.

But, by the time Karl had finally opened and closed the door specially designed to protect the smoking room, ushered Anna through the bar to the smoking room beyond, and indicated she should take a seat on the padded leather bench that ran along the room's perimeter, Anna was rattled to the very marrow of her bones.

Something was going on. Something she was almost certain was going to be unpleasant.

What did Karl want?

He prowled the room restlessly, as if unable to settle, unable to make up his mind as to how to start. But as always, he moved gracefully, his controlled pacing reminding Anna of some caged jungle cat. He kept to the center of the room, avoiding the tables and chairs that ran around its edge.

Anna resisted the temptation to fiddle with the ashtray on the table beside her. To do so would only betray her nervousness. Instead, she kept her hands tightly clasped together in her lap.

He's only toying with me, she thought. *Trying to draw out the suspense, make me suffer.*

For the first time since boarding the *Hindenburg*, Anna felt trapped. She realized how small the passenger area truly was. There was no place she could go to escape from Karl. The air in the smoking room was stale and heavy. Its sour smell clogged Anna's lungs.

Say something, she told herself. *Don't let him see that his tactics are working. Don't let him see how frightened you are.*

"I appreciate privacy as much as the next person," she said. "But don't you think posting a guard outside the door is taking things a bit too far?"

Karl stopped his restless prowling and stared down at her with emotionless eyes. "He is not a guard," he answered, his own voice perfectly calm. "He is simply here to ensure that we are not disturbed, not that anyone is likely to come along. It's too early in the morning. Most of the other passengers are still in bed. Those who have risen are on the deck above us, having their breakfast."

Where I should be, Anna thought. But Karl had planned too well. He'd known she would be up early. It was a habit she'd learned from her grandfather. In spite of the stale air of the smoking room, Anna felt cold.

"Thank you for explaining the situation so clearly," she said. "It makes me feel so much better. Now, what is it that you want from me, Karl?"

In answer, Karl reached into his jacket, withdrew a slim piece of paper and tapped one folded edge of it against his palm. Anna felt her already fraying nerves stretch almost to the breaking point.

"The captain received this communication last night."

"Communication," Anna echoed dully. Her head began to pound.

"From your brother," Karl continued in a flat, emotionless tone. "In it he indicates that you are on this ship against his will and that he has arranged for you to be met upon our landing in Lakehurst, New Jersey, and returned to Germany as soon as possible.

"The *Hindenburg*'s return trip is fully booked. So Kurt asks for the captain's assistance in seeing that his wishes are carried out, that you are put safely into the hands of his representative."

"I see," Anna said, her throat as dry as dust.

Why didn't he just ask you to do it, Karl? But perhaps a Nazi spy is too important to do my brother's dirty work.

"And naturally the captain turned the matter over to you," she said aloud. It was the closest she could come to the taunt she wished to make.

"There is nothing natural about this situation, Anna," Karl answered, his voice abruptly sharp.

So he wasn't as calm as he looked. That was good, Anna thought, though at the moment she could think of no way to use that fact to her own advantage. Her normally quick mind simply wasn't functioning. Her fear was making her dull-witted.

She watched as Karl took a breath to compose himself.

"The captain should not have to be bothered with something of this nature," he continued more calmly. "So I informed him that I was acquainted with you and offered to handle the matter myself."

Then it was over. Everything was over, Anna thought. She could not match wits with Karl and hope to win. Unlike Kurt, Karl knew her too well. Her dream of freedom was over almost before it had begun.

She stared down at the table, struggling against the impulse to shut out the sight of the man who would be the instrument to deprive her of her freedom. With all her heart, she wished to close her eyes.

When she spoke, her tone was light and conversational, as if she was making small talk at a party.

"Do you know what Kurt has planned for me? I am to live in the home of his commanding officer, Colonel Holst, and serve as a companion to the colonel's daughter. When I am judged to be a malleable and proper German maiden, Kurt will find me a suitable husband—"

"Anna," Karl interrupted. But Anna kept on talking. What did it matter if she cut him off? He could do nothing else to hurt her. And soon, too soon now, she would have no more opportunities to speak her mind.

"—and I will spend the rest of my life with a man I have not chosen, a man I do not love. I will live my days according to his will, bearing his children, raising them to believe in the glory of the fatherland, to do their duty to the Third Reich."

Anna lifted her gaze to Karl's. All of a sudden, she was glad she had not closed her eyes. She wanted to look into Karl's directly. Wanted to know he understood what he was doing when he sent her back.

"It will not matter what I think," she continued. "It will not matter *that* I think. And it will not matter what I want. My life will be ruled by the will of my husband. That is the life I ran away from, the life to which you will return me, Karl."

Anna's lips twisted into a bitter smile. "But perhaps I will be fortunate," she said. "Perhaps I will die young, in childbirth."

"You must not say such things, Anna!" Karl burst out, his voice harsh. All of a sudden Anna realized his fists were clenched, the piece of paper carrying her brother's message crushed almost beyond recognition in one of them.

So he does feel something, after all. What is it, I wonder?

Anna no longer felt anything at all. She'd stopped feeling the moment she understood that Karl would see her brother's wishes carried out. He would send her back to Germany.

How can I feel? she thought. Her hope was dead. Her reason for living was gone, the thing that made her feelings possible, that kept her dreams alive.

She rose from her seat and stepped around the table in front of her, her eyes still on Karl's.

"Please, do not concern yourself about me, Karl. You may satisfy yourself that you have done your duty and not look back. You ought to be good at that. You've done it before."

"Stop it, Anna!" Karl ground out. "You have no idea why I—" He broke off, passed a hand across his face.

Anna found she could no longer bear to look into his eyes. She turned away, staring at the wall of the smoking room.

"I did not say that I would carry out your brother's wishes," Karl continued, his voice calmer now. "I merely said that Captain Pruss had agreed to turn the matter over to me."

Anna's composure wobbled as she felt her hope revive. Perhaps he wouldn't send her back after all.

"What do you intend to do, Karl?" She forced herself to turn around, and found herself looking once more into Karl Mueller's unreadable eyes.

Once, Anna had been so sure that she would be the one, the only one, who could read him. The only one who could bring the spark of fire into those ice-blue eyes.

But now she was no longer sure of anything about Karl Mueller. What he felt, if he felt, Anna could no longer tell.

"What happens next will depend on you, Anna," Karl finally replied. "I require a . . . *service*, a task I'd once hoped to perform myself but now find that I cannot. If you will do as I ask, I will see to it that your brother's wishes are not carried out. I will make it possible for you to remain in America, someplace where Kurt will never find you."

Cold sweat broke out over Anna's body. Without warning, her legs refused to hold her. She stumbled back, hand fumbling for the seat behind her, and abruptly sat down.

All the while, her mind was screaming at her, demanding she refuse this thing that Karl was asking, no matter what it cost. Because her mind, so slow only moments before, had instantly leaped to the only logical conclusion.

"You want me to become what you are, don't you?" she whispered. "You want me to become a spy."

10

Karl's face blazed with sudden color, then turned as white as polished bone. His eyes gleamed like hard blue diamonds in his pale face.

Even his lips were white and bloodless, Anna thought. But he did not open them, did not deny the thing that she had called him. The thing that he was asking her to become. And because he did not deny it, Anna knew it was the truth.

"Who is it?" she demanded, her voice strained and harsh. "Who is your—our—intended victim?"

"Erik Peterson," Karl replied.

Bile rose in Anna's throat. She swallowed hard to force it back down.

I suppose I should be grateful it isn't Frau Friedrickson or that nice Ernst couple, she thought. *Oh, Opa! I hope*

*you never knew what Karl was really like. I wish I did
not have to know it now.*

But she did. And because she did, she also knew
she faced a bitter choice. She could do as Karl
asked . . . or she could return to the life Kurt had
planned for her, a life Anna was absolutely certain
would kill her spirit and her mind. But the life Karl
offered might be even worse, because it would be a
life that looked like freedom. Only Anna would know
that it was built upon a lie.

Can I even call it freedom, she wondered, *if to win
it I must sell my soul?*

She became aware of Karl, watching her steadily,
his blue eyes unfathomable as always.

Say something, Anna commanded herself.

"Why Erik Peterson?" she inquired.

"Some of his activities have been suspicious," Karl
answered, beginning to pace around the smoking
room once more. "That is all I can tell you, Anna,
all you really need to know."

"All you *will* tell me, you mean," Anna shot back
before she could help herself. Karl spun back around.
For one split second Anna was sure she recognized
the expression on his face: he was proud of her spirited answer. Then, once more, all expression was
gone.

"I do not need to explain myself to you, Anna,"
Karl said. "In fact, I do not need to make this offer
to you at all. No one would blame me if I simply

did as your brother requested and return you to Germany. He is the head of the household, after all."

I would blame you, Anna thought. *But you no longer care about my feelings.*

She took a deep, unsteady breath. "What do you want me to do?"

"I want Erik Peterson watched. I want to know who he talks to and what he does while he is on board. If he singles anyone out for special attention, either passenger or crew, I want to know that immediately."

Anna took a second breath, steadier this time. "Except for me, of course."

Again for a fraction of a second she thought she saw Karl's eyes widen. But the reaction was over so quickly that she wondered if she'd imagined it.

"Of course," Karl acknowledged. "Erik's obvious preference for your company is one of the reasons you are so perfect for this assignment. That and the fact that you have something to hide."

Not any longer, Anna thought. *You have taken all my secrets, Karl.* She tilted her head back, looked up at him. *How did I ever believe I knew this man, could move him? How did I ever believe I loved him and he loved me?*

Now surely that love was dead.

"You're very good at this, aren't you, Karl?"

The tiniest hint of color crept into his face. "I take my duties seriously, yes," Karl replied.

"And just what are those duties, exactly?" Anna asked, her voice taunting.

Instantly Karl's expression hardened.

"I am not going to explain myself to you, Anna. Not now. Not ever, no matter how much you goad me. So you can stop playing childish games you know you cannot win. Are you going to cooperate or not? A simple one-word answer will suffice," Karl went on, his tone becoming deceptively mild. "You can say yes or no."

Anna clasped her hands together so hard that her nails dug into her palms. *I hate you, Karl Mueller. I hate you with all my heart*, she thought. *Someday I will find a way to pay you back for what you are doing, for what you are making me do.*

"Yes," she whispered.

"I did not hear you," Karl said. "What did you say?"

Anna shot to her feet. "Yes, you unfeeling bastard!" she shouted, using language she'd never used before. "I will do what you ask. I have no choice and you know it. Now let me go."

Unbelievably, Karl grinned at her. "You swear as if you mean it, Anna. Anton would be proud."

White-hot spots of anger danced in Anna's vision. To keep herself from taking a swing at him, Anna clenched her fists at her sides. "You will not mention my grandfather to me, Karl. You dishonor his memory by speaking his name aloud."

For the space of a heartbeat, there was total silence. Karl's face could have been cut from solid stone.

"I hear the reading room is pleasant in the late afternoon," he finally said, in a voice that sent chills rippling along Anna's spine. "Say, perhaps, to write a letter. Four o'clock would be a good time. One could even have a cup of tea."

Oh, yes, you are very good at this, Anna thought. Surely only someone completely ruthless could change gears so rapidly.

"I will remember that," she said. "Four o'clock."

"Excellent," Karl said. "Then I will say good morning."

Anna didn't wait for a second signal that she was free to go. Forcing herself to move slowly, her back straight, she walked from the smoking room through the bar.

I ran away from you, once, she thought, *just as I loved you once. Once. But no more.*

She reached out to open the airlock door. But in her agitation she couldn't work the mechanism. The door stayed closed. Abruptly, panic swept through Anna. A hot band of fear tightened around her chest. She felt the walls of the small bar grow closer. Too close.

"Let me out," she gasped. "You said that I could go. You can't keep me here against my will! Let me out, Karl."

Instantly, Karl moved to stand beside her. "It's not locked, Anna. You just don't know how to open the door. But I can't do it if you're standing there. You'll have to step back."

He placed a hand on her arm. At the feel of his fingers wrapped around her forearm, Anna lost her fragile hold on her self-control. She turned toward him, swinging out blindly. She felt her open palm connect in a sharp slap.

Karl released her, and Anna staggered away. Absolute silence fell over the bar. Then Anna became aware that she could hear someone gasping, struggling for breath. *It's me*, she thought. She raised her tingling hand to press it against her aching chest, then turned to look at Karl.

Karl stood with his face averted, staring at the closed door. With a jolt, Anna realized that she could see his shoulders rising and falling rapidly, as if he too was struggling for breath.

Then he moved, his fingers working the door mechanism. Anna heard a hiss of air as the door was released and swung open. Without a word, Karl stepped back. Anna stumbled forward. His eyes still straight ahead, as if staring at nothing, the crewman outside stepped aside to let her pass.

For the rest of her life, Anna never knew what made her do it. One moment she was facing forward, toward what little freedom the *Hindenburg* now offered. The next moment she was turning back, toward where Karl stood framed in the doorway. There was nothing to show Anna what he was feeling. *If* he was feeling. But slanting across one cheek, as red and angry as an open wound, Anna could see the imprint of her own palm. For the rest of her life, she knew she would carry the image of her handprint emblazoned across Karl's pale face.

Against all thought, against all reason, Anna felt her heart wrench once.

Then she turned around and walked away.

There has to be a way out of this, and I have to find it.

Alone once more in the relative safety of her cabin, Anna paced. Walking back and forth, back and forth, across the pale gray carpet, she tried to calm her agitated nerves enough to do the thing her grandfather had taught her, the thing she knew she should have done in the first place: use her head.

She'd been unable to think while she was face to face with Karl Mueller. He had the ability to make her focus solely on him, just as he always had. Anna had found that ability exciting, once. Now she found that it simply frightened her.

But even Karl is human, she thought, as she took another fruitless turn around her cabin. *There has to be a flaw in his plan somewhere. I haven't been able to see it yet. But I will.*

But after two solid hours of pacing, Anna was exhausted, and she had nothing to show for her efforts except sore feet and a headache. She could visit the ship's doctor for a cure, but he had no cure for the thing that had brought them on in the first place.

Finally even Anna was forced to admit the truth: she could find no way out of the trap Karl had sprung upon her. Karl knew her well enough to use the desires of her heart against her.

Thoroughly discouraged, Anna gave up pacing and collapsed onto her bunk. *Perhaps I should just pretend to be ill for the rest of the journey.* She certainly felt ill enough at the moment. Never could she recall so fierce a headache.

Pleading illness would never work, though. Normally she was healthy—the only trait she possessed of which her brother had ever approved. But here again the fact that Karl knew Anna so well would work against her. He would never believe she was too sick to leave her cabin.

Anna could just imagine him showing up once more at her cabin door, forcing her to go in search of Erik Peterson. Would he drag her out by her hair next time? she wondered. Or perhaps he would order her from her room at gunpoint.

At the ridiculous images, Anna snorted. *I was wrong,* she thought. *I haven't lost everything. I still have what passes for my sense of humor.* She leaned back on the pillow and closed her aching eyes.

Her grandfather's voice rang in her head: "Go lie

down, Anna. Look at the situation from a different angle."

It was his favorite way of solving puzzles. *I'm trying, Opa,* Anna thought. Then she caught her breath as an image materialized in her mind, almost as if she'd summoned it.

It was an image of Karl's face, as they'd stood together in line at the Frankfurter Hof. Once more Anna saw the look on Karl's face when he saw Erik drape one arm casually across her shoulder. Again she saw the quick flash in Karl's eyes. The tightening of his jaw that was the surest sign that he was angry.

Karl had hated Erik's gesture, Anna thought. Resented the fact that she'd given permission for another man to touch her. Only he should have the right to do that, it seemed, even if he didn't want her.

Anna's eyes flew open. That was it, she thought, and felt her headache begin to ease and her spirits lighten for the first time since striking her devil's bargain.

Karl had beaten her by using her own desires against her. But that didn't mean she had to roll over and play dead for him. She hadn't found a way out, but she had found a weapon to use in her own defense. And Karl himself had shown her the way to use it against him.

He'd beaten her because he knew her so well. But he had forgotten that Anna also knew him. She could read the signals that told her Karl didn't like her relationship with Erik, even as he asked her to pursue it.

Anna felt her headache vanish completely. Surprised and delighted by the sudden shift her mood had taken, she sat up and actually grinned. There was no need to hide in her cabin, no need to hide from Erik Peterson. In fact, there was every reason to seek him out, spend every possible moment with him, not to accomplish Karl's ends but to accomplish her own.

I'll see where my attraction to Erik leads, Anna decided.

And she'd make absolutely certain Karl knew she was enjoying every moment of it.

"Whoa! Slow down, Anna!"

Energized by her decision, Anna had dashed from her cabin and headed for the dining room. Now that a hard ball of tension no longer filled her stomach, she had realized how hungry she was. She would have breakfast, then go in search of Erik.

But as she reached the landing by the staircase, she'd barreled directly into him. The force of their contact rocked them both backward. Erik reacted instantly, instinctively, his arms coming up to hold her.

Again Anna felt the familiar rush of heat. *I'd have recognized this anywhere,* she thought. *Recognized him.*

She almost told him.

It would feel so good to lean against him, just for a moment, to confide the part she was about to play, the terrible thing she had been forced to promise. If the Nazis were suspicious of him, surely Erik was someone it was safe to trust.

She kept silent only because she didn't know Erik well enough to predict how he would react. She'd been drawn to the impulsive acceptance of her challenge that had led him to help her board.

But if Erik challenged Karl, if he went to him with what Anna told him, she would lose her only chance to be free of the life Kurt had chosen for her. She would lose everything.

I don't really know Erik at all, in fact, she thought, as she lifted her head to stare up at him. *I only know how much I want to know him.* Karl had tried to poison even that, but Anna didn't have to let him do it.

Erik's gypsy eyes looked down at her, the smile in them not quite hiding their sharpness.

"What's the matter, afraid you'll miss breakfast?" he asked in a teasing voice. "I'm surprised you didn't get up earlier. I wouldn't have pegged you for a slugabed, Anna."

If you only knew, Anna thought. *Well, here goes nothing.*

She gave a breathless little laugh. "I'm not so late usually," she admitted. "I guess, with all the excitement of yesterday, I overslept."

"Well, you must come along and eat something now," Erik said, tucking her arm into the crook of his elbow as he turned toward the dining room.

Anna felt her whole body begin to relax. She'd

crossed the first hurdle, explaining away her morning absence. In spite of his clever green eyes, Erik had accepted her excuse without question.

"Frau Friedrickson will want to see you, I know," Erik continued, "and then I have a surprise for you, Anna."

Anna stopped, uncertain whether to be delighted or alarmed. "A surprise. What is it?"

Erik laughed under his breath. "It's a *surprise*," he answered. "If I tell you, I'll ruin it. You can't know everything, Anna."

Anna stopped dead. Goose bumps rose on her skin. "What did you just say?" she asked.

Her abrupt halt pulled Erik up short. He looked down at her, his expression alert and curious. "I said, if I tell you about the surprise, then you'll know what it is," he answered. "I can't tell you every-thing, Anna."

That's it, Anna thought. *That's the answer*.

What had Karl said, just that morning? "That is all that I can tell you, Anna, all you need to know."

At the time, Anna had been too distressed and distracted to recognize the statement's implications. But she was thinking clearly now.

I'm finally using my head, Opa.

The way out of her cage was so close, she hadn't recognized it. For the second time that morning, Anna felt herself grinning.

You think I am at your mercy, Karl, she thought, *when just the opposite is true.*

"I don't want you to tell me everything," she answered Erik, her heart singing. She gave his hand a tug and moved at a brisk pace toward the dining room. "I love surprises. But first I need some breakfast."

I see my way out now, she thought. *The way to turn the tables.*

She would report on the time she spent with Erik in great detail, and she would tell Karl Mueller absolutely nothing.

The surprise was a tour of the airship. Anna hadn't known such a thing was possible, but Erik assured her it was easy to arrange.

"All you need to do is ask for one," he said, as he and Anna walked downstairs to B deck. "The chief steward usually conducts them, though last year the captain led many of the tours himself. I'm not sure who it will be this—"

"Good morning. I apologize for keeping you waiting," a voice said.

I should have known, Anna thought.

Karl Mueller was going to be their tour guide.

At the sight of Karl, Erik's dark eyebrows shot up. Anna was standing just close enough to feel a quiver of some emotion pass through his body. But his face gave no hint of what that emotion might be. And even Anna could not read Karl's face.

He clicked his heels together smartly. "Karl Mueller, at your service," he said, bowing slightly. "Captain Pruss sends his apologies, but his duties prevent him from conducting your tour himself. Instead, he has asked me to take you this morning."

So that's the way it is to be, Anna thought. *He's going to pretend he doesn't know us.*

The fact that Karl could do so with so little effort sent unease prickling through her. Unease and something that felt suspiciously like pain.

If he can pretend so easily now, he could have done so before, she thought. *It's true, then. I've never really known him.*

"But that is excellent," Erik said, his tone hearty. If a game was being played, it was plain he was going to do his part.

"We have met before, haven't we?" Erik went on. "In the lobby of the Frankfurter Hof? But I don't think we were properly introduced." He bowed in his turn, then straightened and extended his hand. "Erik Peterson."

Anna watched as Karl's arm came up, his hand clasped Erik's. On both sides, the grip was tight, as if each was testing the strength of the other. Anna could almost feel a message pass between them, a warning and a challenge.

I don't understand any of this, she thought—and was

surprised to discover her own emotion. For the first time, she realized that she was angry.

Then Erik loosened his grip, dropped his hand, and touched her elbow lightly. "I believe you are acquainted with my companion, Fraulein Anna Becker?" he said, his tone making it a question.

"Indeed," Karl answered, his blue eyes flicking over Anna. "I am an old friend of Fraulein Becker's family."

It was the same claim Erik had made in line at the Frankfurter Hof. Only this time it was true.

"Then you need no introduction," Erik said.

Karl inclined his head ever so slightly.

"If you will follow me—but I forget," he said, cutting himself off in midsentence. "I am sorry, but I must make certain that you are not wearing anything metal. Fraulein, you are not wearing any jewelry?"

"No," Anna answered, mystified by the question.

To her astonishment, Karl knelt at her feet. "If you will permit me?"

He lifted one foot, examined her shoe. "Ah," he said. "I must ask you to remove your shoes, fraulein," he said, rising once more, "and wear these."

Anna looked down at the shoes Karl had produced. They were flat soled, the tops made of heavy canvas. Anna felt a spurt of irritation surge through her. Was this some new game Karl was playing? "What for?" she asked a little waspishly.

Karl opened his mouth to speak, but Erik was too quick for him.

"Your buckles, Anna," he said quietly.

Anna looked down at the tiny silver buckles on her stylish shoes. "My buckles?" she echoed.

Karl hissed his breath out through his teeth. Erik made an exclamation. "Can it be that you do not realize what it is that keeps this great silver beast aloft, my sweet Anna?" Erik explained.

"Of course I know what keeps us aloft," Anna snapped irritably. "It's . . ." Her mind went blank. What had her grandfather said?

"It's hydrogen," Erik filled in softly. "A regrettably flammable substance. One spark from your shiny buckles striking against a metal catwalk and we could all go up in flames."

Anna felt her scalp begin to prickle. She had no recollection of her grandfather telling her this, no idea that such a thing was even possible.

"But I've been wearing them all morning," she protested. "And besides, there's a *smoking* room—" She broke off, appalled. She'd been in the smoking room only once—with Karl that morning.

"You've been wearing your shoes in carpeted areas," Karl answered calmly. "When we go into the body of the ship, we will be walking among the hydrogen cells, so we must take extra precautions.

"The smoking room is sealed with a special airlock door, and no matches are used inside it; cigarettes are lit with a special electric lighter. Even the reporters on board are not allowed to carry their cameras, fraulein: one flash from a bulb . . ." Karl let his voice trail off.

Well, I guess he's qualified to give the tour, Anna thought. *He certainly seems to know what he's talking about.*

"If you will allow me, fraulein," Karl said after another moment.

He knelt once more, then wrapped one strong hand around her ankle and lifted her foot. To keep her balance, Anna braced herself with one hand against his shoulder and was all but overwhelmed by a flood of powerful memories. They'd been in this position once before.

No! she thought. *I won't remember.* But the memories continued to pour through her. She was powerless to stop them.

They'd gone ice-skating one cold winter day, a day just like the one on which he'd said good-bye to her. And Karl had knelt just as he was kneeling now, to help Anna put her skates on. But then he'd stood up so quickly that Anna had lost her balance. To keep her from falling, Karl had pulled her into his arms. In the next moment he'd told her for the first time that he loved her. . . .

"Your shoes will be returned to your cabin during our tour, fraulein," he said now, as he released the foot that he'd been holding. He exchanged the shoe on her other foot swiftly, but when he was finished, he was careful to rise slowly. There would be no chance for Anna to lose her balance this time.

He remembers, too, Anna thought. *He remembers all the lies.* She couldn't bring herself to look at him.

"And your shoes, Herr Peterson?" Karl asked in an expressionless voice.

"I have come prepared, as you see," Erik answered. Anna looked down at his feet. For the first time, she noticed that his shoes were made entirely of leather, even the tips of his shoelaces. Not even the grommets for the laces were made of metal.

Abruptly Anna felt the very air around her change. She could almost feel the tension crackle against her face. Against her will, her eyes shot to Karl. What on earth was happening?

"It would seem you know the *Hindenburg* well," Karl said.

Erik shrugged, but his green eyes were dancing. "I have a general interest in aviation. I took the tour several times last year, so I knew what precautions to take. It is a very big ship, is it not?"

There was a moment of charged silence. Anna felt the tension rise until she feared it might choke her.

"But Anna has not seen it yet," Erik said.

Karl smiled then, a movement of his lips that was entirely without mirth or warmth.

"Then let us show her," he said.

An hour later Anna wished she'd never left her cabin. Instead, she was standing on the axial catwalk, an aluminum walkway that ran the entire length of the airship, right down the *Hindenburg*'s very center.

Now Anna truly felt as if she were in the belly of a whale. The great gas cells surrounded her.

But before they entered the body of the airship, Karl had taken them into the control car, the nerve center of the *Hindenburg*. Anna had seen the telephone switchboard that enabled the captain to speak to other stations in the ship, the navigation room with its charts, the rudder and elevator stations, standing at right angles to each another. Both areas were manned around the clock.

The vertical rudders, emblazoned with enormous swastikas, moved the ship from side to side. But it was the "elevators," the ends of the horizontal fins, that guided the vessel up and down.

And it was the elevator man, standing parallel to the centerline of the ship, who was responsible for the smooth ride she was enjoying, Karl informed Anna. From his post, he could sense any change in the angle of the airship and correct it immediately.

"Thank you," Anna had told the serious young man standing there, and been rewarded when he smiled.

Karl had also shown them the radio room, which was also manned twenty-four hours a day.

What a fool I was, Anna thought, *to think we were out of touch and I was safe, simply because we were airborne.*

In front and just above the control car were the officers' quarters. Freight rooms stretched across and above that area. Behind it were the mail room and some fuel and water tanks. Karl had shown her all of them.

Anna had found it fascinating, but as she entered the body of the airship, she'd begun to feel alarmed. Here she was completely surrounded by the hydrogen gas cells that ran from one end of the ship to the other, sixteen in all. The deeper into the *Hindenburg* they moved, the more overwhelmed Anna became. She felt like a small animal burrowing deeper and deeper into a never-ending hole.

Each gas cell fit into its own metal compartment, which also provided the airship's rigid outer structure. The cells were protected from rubbing against their housing by cotton partitions between the cells and by net covers, like hot-air balloons.

Riggers constantly monitored the pressure in the cells. An experienced man could estimate a cell's pressure just by placing his hand on it as he walked by. A tight cell meant high pressure; a loose cell, low pressure.

"Why don't they use a gas that is less dangerous than hydrogen?" Anna asked now. They were walking along the length of the ship toward the tail. Anna could still hardly believe she was surrounded by a substance that she couldn't see but that could be so deadly.

"Because no other gas is readily available," Karl answered.

"The Americans use helium in their zeppelins," Erik commented.

"True," Karl said swiftly. "But if you know that much, you must also know that the supply is limited and that the Americans control it. No one uses helium without their permission."

Anna's mind quickly filled in what Karl hadn't said: The Americans had withheld the gas from Germany, probably because they found the führer's policies alarming.

"Why use hydrogen at all if it's so dangerous?" she asked.

"It's very buoyant," Karl answered, "and it's only dangerous under certain conditions. It doesn't become flammable until it's combined with oxygen. As long as the gas cells remain intact, we are perfectly safe."

Nevertheless, Anna shuddered.

"Let us go back," Karl said at once. He swung himself out onto the rubber-runged ladder leading down to the keel catwalk. "I'll go first. Please follow me, fraulein."

Still the perfect tour guide, Anna thought. Only during their meeting this morning, when they were alone, had Karl called her Anna.

Anna stuck one leg out, felt with her foot for the first rung of the ladder, then put her weight on it. She began to climb down, carefully keeping her eyes straight ahead. A few moments later Erik joined them.

He hadn't spoken much during the tour. But

then, he'd seen it all before, several times, Anna remembered.

Why had he asked to see the ship again now? Was it because of the strange thing happening between Erik and Karl, or was it solely for Anna's pleasure and benefit?

Something was going on between the two men, Anna was almost sure of it. Something she was equally sure had nothing to do with her. She'd just had the misfortune to end up in the middle.

I'm tired of thinking about it, she thought, as her feet touched the lower catwalk. *Tired of this whole mess. Tired of everything.*

She knew her grandfather would not have approved of her attitude. But for the first time since Anton Becker's death, Anna found herself trying not to think about him.

Everything had been so much simpler, so much better, when her grandfather was with her. Would Anna have been in this impossible position if her grandfather were still alive?

Opa would never have approved of that kind of thinking, either, she thought, realizing that she'd failed utterly in her effort not to think about him. He'd always been a realist.

A realist with a sense of wonder, Anna amended. It was one of the things she'd loved best about him.

She stepped away from the ladder and stared back up into the ship. With its multiple catwalks, webbing, and cross-braces, the interior of the *Hindenburg* looked for all the world like a fantastical construction made with a child's toy building set.

Oh, Opa, how I wish you had made this journey with me. You would have loved this.

In spite of all her efforts to the contrary, she felt tears filling her eyes.

"Is something wrong?" Karl asked.

"No," Anna answered, blinking rapidly to force back the tears. Behind her she heard Erik reach the bottom of the ladder and step out onto the catwalk. "I was just thinking how much my grandfather would have loved to see this."

"Anna . . ." Karl took a step toward her, and without thinking, Anna quickly stepped back.

Too quickly. Her foot slipped off the catwalk.

Anna's ears rang in sudden panic. She felt herself tilting at a dangerous angle, straight out into the open air beneath the keel catwalk. Her hands scrabbled for some kind of hold, but met only emptiness.

She was falling!

She couldn't prevent it, could find nothing to stop her from tumbling over.

"Anna!"

She heard her name shouted, as if from a great distance, but she couldn't respond. It seemed to Anna that time itself had changed in the second since her foot had slipped from the catwalk, moving more and more slowly. She felt like a sleepwalker.

Then she became aware that strong arms were lifting her, standing her upright, but she couldn't tell to whom they belonged. For one moment she thought she might suffocate, because she couldn't catch her breath. She was surrounded. There were too many arms around her, as if the three of them were one. Anna felt their strange bulk sway from side to side.

Then time resumed its normal course with a horrible, brutal snap—and it was Karl, not Anna, who was tumbling over.

Anna opened her mouth to scream, but no sound came out. She strained forward, but she couldn't move. Erik's arms were too tight around her.

"Hold still," he said, his voice a rough rasp in her ear. "The drop isn't far, and the outer skin is strong. It will be all right, Anna. He won't be harmed."

Anna watched as Karl bounced against the skin of the great zeppelin once, twice. At any moment she expected the outer covering to tear and Karl to disappear through it. But the fabric skin held.

"He's not going to go through!" she cried in wonder.

Erik's arms loosened just a fraction. "I told you no harm would come to him, Anna. I've seen the captain jump down himself, just to show how strong the outer skin is. Look, now. He's coming back."

Karl had clambered to his feet and was moving with great care back toward the catwalk. He swung himself up onto it, then stood still for a moment, leaning against one of the braces. He appeared perfectly composed, but Anna could see the pulse beat rapidly in his throat.

Finally Karl lifted his head. Anna felt those deep blue eyes upon her, and knew that she couldn't hold her feelings inside for much longer. She pulled free of Erik's arms with a quick jerk.

"I've seen enough for one day," she said, not allowing herself to care how horrible she sounded. If she cared about that, she would have to care about so much more. Too much.

"As far as I'm concerned, this tour is over," she added.

13

"I'm very pleased to see you, my dear. I was beginning to think you'd fallen overboard."

At Frau Friedrickson's words, Anna repressed a quick shudder. Her friend's jest was uncomfortably close to Anna's horror at what had happened on the tour that morning. It had taken her all afternoon to regain her composure.

Anna hadn't been proud of the fact that she'd stayed in her cabin for the rest of the day, though she had stopped short of burying her head beneath the covers. But the alternative had felt even worse. She simply could not bring herself to face anyone until she had her emotions in control. And that meant sorting out her troubled feelings for Karl Mueller.

Anna had been horrified at the thought that Karl might have been hurt on their tour this morning or, even worse, that he might have been lost forever. But she'd been equally horrified at the power of her own emotions.

She couldn't allow herself to give in to her feelings for Karl, particularly not now that he had such a terrible hold over her.

But the quiet afternoon, though it had calmed Anna's nerves, hadn't really helped her solve her problem. By the time she dressed for dinner, Anna was forced to admit that her feelings for Karl were just as confused as ever. Even the dress she chose to wear reflected her mood. It was a pale gray, almost the same color as her cabin.

Finally, annoyed with herself, Anna resolutely vowed not to think about Karl any longer. After tonight there would be just one more day of travel before the *Hindenburg* reached America. One more day of freedom before it all might be over. Surely she ought to have been wondering what Karl would do if she had nothing to report by the time they landed. That was more important than her feelings for him, wasn't it?

"I wasn't feeling well this afternoon," Anna told Frau Friedrickson now, happy she could tell the truth. "So I spent a few hours in my cabin."

"But that is so unfortunate," Frau Friedrickson cried at once. "If I had known, I would have looked in on you, my dear, since our cabins are right across from each other. I hope you are better now."

"Much," Anna said. And was surprised to discover that she meant it. Being out among the other passengers was providing a distraction.

She and Frau Friedrickson were seated at one of the larger dinner tables that evening. The girl about her own age whom Anna had noticed right before she boarded the *Hindenburg* was sitting beside them.

Anna had tried to speak to the young woman, but every time she'd done so, her father had answered for her. Plainly, he was training his daughter to be a proper German young lady, and that meant not speaking to anyone she didn't know.

"What do you say we take our coffee into the lounge this evening," Frau Friedrickson suggested as the waiter cleared their plates away. "I hear that fellow who brought on the dog is an entertainer. He's going to play the piano, which is made of aluminum and pigskin, so it would not be too heavy, I suppose. Can you imagine that?"

Anna pulled her attention away from the girl at her side. "On this ship I can imagine anything," she said. And was rewarded by the tinkling sound of Frau Friedrickson's laughter. The older woman pushed her chair back and got to her feet just as a shadow fell across the table.

"Ladies," a smooth voice said, "might I hope that you are going to the lounge and that I might be permitted to escort you?"

Anna felt her heart rate quicken.

"With manners like that, young man," Frau Friedrickson answered before Anna could speak, "anything is possible." She looked over at Anna, her eyes twinkling. "What do you say, my dear? Shall we grant this young man's request?"

Anna felt her spirits lighten. An evening of flirtation would be just the thing to take her mind off her problems.

"By all means," she said, and slipped her arm through Erik Peterson's.

An hour later Anna was more relaxed than she'd been all day, seated in the lounge with Erik and Frau Friedrickson. Erik had brought her a glass of sparkling wine, a luxury Anna seldom indulged in.

She was careful not to drink too much, but the bubbles in the drink still tickled her nose and made her feel just a little light-headed.

She could feel Erik's arm, where it rested on the back of her chair, close to but not quite touching her skin.

The man Anna had seen playing the piano last night turned out to be the owner of the dog. His real name was Joseph Spah. But as a performer he was known as Ben Dova. Usually he performed as an acrobat.

"Play something German," one of the passengers called out now. Without missing a beat, Spah swung into a spirited polka. A ripple of delighted laughter ran through the lounge.

Without warning, Anna felt Erik's warm fingers pressed against her back. She looked up, a question in her eyes.

"Dance with me, Anna."

Instantly, all Anna's fears about calling attention to herself came rushing back. "No, Erik, I can't. I musn't."

"What do you mean, you can't?" he inquired, rising to his feet. "Of course you can. Every good German girl knows how to polka."

"Erik," Anna protested once more as he pulled her to her feet. But her heart stumbled as he pulled her close.

"No more arguments," he whispered. "I want my arms around you. Dance with me, Anna."

Out the lounge doorway, down the promenade, then into the far doorway, Erik kept time with the music, turning her in the brisk, tight circles of the polka. By the time she and Erik completed their circuit twice, Anna was breathless with laughter. Her head spun with colors—the rich red carpet, the yellow piano, but most of all, the jewel-green intensity of Erik's eyes as he gazed down at her, promising her something.

What? Anna wanted to say. *What do you promise?*

But she couldn't; she was too out of breath. Then, with a final chord for flourish, the polka was over. Passengers in the lounge burst into applause. Laughing under his breath, Erik captured Anna's hand in his, raised it to his lips, then tugged her into a curtsy while he bowed before their audience.

"How charming," Anna heard a woman comment. "Such a striking couple."

"If that piano player has any compassion, he'll play that young man a waltz next time," answered her companion.

Erik laughed softly once more. As if on cue, Anna heard the strains of a waltz drift from the piano.

"Erik," she whispered as his arm encircled her waist. "People are staring."

"Of course they're staring," Erik answered. "I can hardly keep my eyes off you. You are beautiful, Anna."

Without another word he turned her in one slow circle of the waltz, then swept her out of the lounge.

Down the length of the promenade, past the lounge, into the far corner by the reading room they waltzed, till the sound of the piano was a series of muted chords behind them.

In the corner, Erik slowed his steps. The circles in which he moved Anna grew tighter and tighter until finally he stopped moving altogether. But his arm stayed, warm and tight, against her back.

"I've been wanting something else, Anna."

Anna tilted her head back, let her eyes gaze directly into his. She knew what was coming, and she felt her pulse beat in double time at the thought of it.

"I wonder what that could be," she said.

She saw that devil-may-care smile touch his lips right before he lowered his head to kiss her.

Anna felt a hot flush sweep her skin, felt her blood pump, then rush, then run molten. Erik's lips against her mouth were like a brand, marking her, claiming her, burning away every thought of Karl Mueller.

Then, just for a second, he pulled back, his mouth no more than a breath away from hers.

"No," Anna whispered. She fisted her hands in the lapels of his coat, desperate to bring him back, wild to have him closer. She didn't want to stop. Didn't want to go back to what had been. Not tonight. Not ever. "No, Erik. Don't stop. I don't want you to."

She saw his lips part as he drew in a swift breath, and then they were on hers once more, devouring her.

This time Anna was ready as the hot punch of desire speared through her body. She let herself ride the crest of the wave, unafraid of where it might take her.

All that mattered was that she was free. Free, even though Erik's arms were tight around her. She was dimly aware that he'd finally raised his head, tilted her chin up.

"Anna."

"Hmmm," she murmured. It was all she could manage. Her lips felt full and swollen.

"We'd better go back," Erik said, "before I discover I want more."

Anna discovered that her lips could do something else. They could curve into the smile of a seductress.

"Then by all means, let us go back," she said, tucking her hand into the crook of his elbow. "But I think you should know that my grandfather raised me to use my head. I'm always interested in new discoveries."

Erik gave a shout of laughter. As they passed back by the reading room, Anna caught a glint of white. Her footsteps stumbled. Instantly Erik's other arm came around her.

"I'd better be more careful," he said teasingly. "Perhaps my kisses are too powerful."

"Perhaps," Anna said.

Or perhaps she'd just caught a glimpse of the fine, pale hair she'd only ever seen on Karl Mueller.

Anna's legs were still wobbly as she walked to her cabin. In the comparative privacy of the B deck landing, she'd said good night to Erik with a series of kisses that had left her knees weak and her nerves humming.

I don't know whether I'm coming or going, she thought, as she climbed back up the stairs. Then she laughed at herself as she headed for the cabin corridor. *It's just as well, since I don't know where I'll end up.*

"I hope the joke is a good one, Anna."

Anna jumped, one hand moving to the racing pulse at her throat. Karl stood in the hall, just across from her cabin.

"I'm sorry," he said when he saw her reaction. "I didn't mean to startle you."

Anna's already weak knees threatened to buckle. A spurt of anger helped her stand her ground. "I don't believe you. I think you enjoy sneaking up on people, especially me."

She heard rather than saw Karl exhale a quick, irritated breath. "Don't be ridiculous, Anna. And keep your voice down. The walls in this part of the ship are thin."

"What do you want, Karl?" Anna asked more quietly, beginning to feel like a broken record. She'd asked him that this morning, and look where it had gotten her.

"You didn't keep our four o'clock appointment," Karl said. "We had an agreement."

Anna bit her tongue to keep her acid words from spilling out. *No, we did not have an* agreement. *An agreement is something you enter into of your own free will.*

"I wasn't feeling well," she answered shortly. "I stayed in my cabin."

"That's no excuse, Anna."

Anna felt the rest of her temper slip from her control. "Stop treating me like a child. I have a mind, Karl."

"Then use it," Karl hissed harshly. "Because you stayed in your cabin, Peterson was free all afternoon. He was unwatched."

"How can you know he would have spent the time with me even if I'd left my cabin?" Anna countered. "I cannot force him to dance attendance on me."

Karl made a sound of sheer disgust. "You're not stupid, Anna," he said, "so stop pretending to be. From what I saw tonight, I imagine you could have convinced Peterson to spend the afternoon with you without too much difficulty."

So it was you in the reading room, Anna thought. *And you were not just spying on Erik. You were spying on me.*

She took a step toward him, her anger making her lose all caution. "And what about the rest of tonight, Karl? Doesn't that have you worried? Perhaps you want me to go back to Erik now and beg him to spend the night with me. It should take me all night long to give him all the things you showed you didn't want the day you walked away from me."

A ripple of movement passed through Karl's body. Anna felt her breath choke off. She stepped back abruptly.

Never had she seen so much emotion controlled so brutally. Anna felt her own body tense, getting ready to flee. But Karl never moved, and when he spoke, his voice was icy.

"What I want is for you to fulfill your part of our bargain. I'm not playing games, Anna. Stop playing with me."

"And if I spend time with Erik and see nothing?" Anna managed.

"Deciding what is nothing is up to me." He stepped forward, slid the door to her cabin open. "Now you'd better go in," he said. "I know you'll want your beauty sleep, so you can look your best for Peterson tomorrow."

Anna felt her pulse begin to roar inside her head. He hadn't stepped clear of the doorway. There was no way she could enter it without touching him.

"Move out of the way, Karl."

"What's the matter, Anna? Are you afraid of me?"

No, Anna thought desperately. *No, I'm not afraid. And I'm not afraid to prove it.* She started forward.

She was almost to the doorway before Karl stopped her. He stepped forward; Anna stepped back. But the hallway was so narrow she bumped into Frau Friedrickson's closed door just opposite. She could feel the door latch, pressing against her back.

Karl's arms came up on either side of her, pinning her in place.

"*Are* you afraid of me, Anna?"

Karl's blue eyes were intent on her face, an expression in them she'd never seen before.

"Answer me, Anna."

I can't, Anna thought. *I don't know the answer.*

Desperately she licked her dry lips. She heard Karl groan low in his throat. And then his mouth was on hers.

Anna felt the impact of Karl's kiss slam through her body. His touch had always had the power to send her reeling, but even he had never kissed her like this before.

This was a kiss to revel in, to drown in, to die

and be reborn in all at the same time. She could feel his anger, hot and potent as his teeth scraped against hers. His longing, as he used his tongue to tease her lips and ease her mouth more fully open.

Anna's heart sang. It roared. It pounded. Her whole world narrowed to the feel of Karl's lips moving over hers.

"Don't be afraid of me, Anna," he murmured against them. "Don't be. Don't be."

And suddenly Anna knew the answer.

I'm not afraid, she thought. *I couldn't be. Not ever. How is it possible that you don't know that?*

But fear spiked through her then. More powerful even than desire. Wildly, Anna twisted, pushing Karl away, and stumbled across the hall to her cabin. Once inside, she pressed one shaking hand to her tingling lips.

What would have become of her if she'd said those thoughts aloud? She would have been lost. Lost forever.

And worst of all, she would have no one but herself to blame.

"Anna—" Karl started.

"Touch me again and I'll tell Erik everything," she gasped. Then she slid the cabin door shut in his face.

15

She was falling.

Tumbling over and over again from the very top of the great airship as the enormous gas cells pressed in on all sides around her. The force of her fall was so great that she knew she would go through when she hit the bottom. The outer skin wouldn't save her as it had saved Karl. It would refuse to hold her.

She would plunge through into open air, her frantic attempts to save herself rupturing gas cells, mixing oxygen with the deadly, flammable hydrogen.

She would die. They would all die.

Anna sat up in bed, her heart pounding.

She stared at the soothing gray walls of her tiny cabin, willing her pulse rate to slow down. *It was a dream*, she thought. *Only a dream*. With trembling fingers, she reached for her robe and pulled it on over her nightgown.

Then she climbed slowly out of bed, pulled down the sink, and splashed her face with bracing, cold water

I'm too wound up, that's all, she thought. Her once bright future now seemed clouded and uncertain.

I've got to get out of here, she thought. She shrugged out of her nightgown and robe, dressing with haste in whatever was on top of her suitcase, hardly paying attention to what it was, not really caring what she put on.

A moment later Anna was moving down the deserted corridor. All around her the ship felt quiet, the deep steady hum of the engines the only sound. Once again Anna was up before virtually anyone else.

Good, she thought. The last thing she wanted at the moment was company. Anna let her feet guide her toward the stairs that led to the port side of B deck, beneath the dining room. Like the promenade above it, this section of B deck had a bank of windows looking down. But here Anna would be less likely to encounter any other passengers, unless someone wanted an early morning shower.

"What took you so long?"

Startled, Anna pulled up short. That was Erik's voice! But he couldn't be speaking to her. He couldn't see her. She was still standing on the staircase. He was on B deck, below.

"I came as quickly as I could," a second voice said.

"I told you security is tight this trip." The voice sounded a little breathless, as if the speaker had been running.

Who was Erik talking to? Anna wondered.

One part of her mind told her she should simply turn back, pretend she hadn't heard Erik's voice. But another part reminded her that she'd promised to report anything unusual in Erik's behavior.

Was there something unusual about this early morning encounter? Casting a quick glance around to be certain no one else was watching, Anna crept farther down.

"It doesn't matter," she heard Erik say as she got closer. "You're here now." Then his voice dropped too low for Anna to hear anything else. Frustrated, she stopped and considered her options.

This is ridiculous, she told herself. Anna felt terrified and incredibly foolish all at the same time. *What exactly do you think you're doing?* But her quick mind was ready with an answer: *You're spying on him, Anna.*

But did she have good cause?

Her heart pounded. There was only one way to find out: she would have to learn who Erik's companion was and overhear more of their conversation. But how?

This is ridiculous, Anna thought once more. *Don't do it.* But still she took a deep breath to steady herself. Then she moved noiselessly down the rest of the stairs. Standing on the very bottom step, she gripped the banister and leaned out to peek around the corner.

Erik stood at the end of the short hallway, near the entrance to the shower room. His back was toward her. Anna still couldn't see his companion. Erik's stance blocked him. But that meant he couldn't see Anna, either, even though he was facing in her direction.

Then the second man gestured with one arm and Anna felt her senses sharpen. She recognized that color. She'd seen it once before, on her tour of the airship yesterday morning. It belonged to the special coveralls the men wore while working inside the ship. Like the shoes Anna had worn on the tour, the coveralls had no metal on them anywhere, not even the shanks of the buttons.

Anna's heart slammed against her ribs in painful rhythm. That could mean only one thing, she realized: Erik was talking to a zeppelin crewman.

Anna jerked her head back around the corner. She gripped the banister so tightly her knuckles turned white.

Stop being foolish, she told herself fiercely. *There's probably a perfectly reasonable explanation.*

The trouble was, she couldn't think of one at the moment. And this was exactly the sort of behavior Karl had wanted her to watch for.

Had he been right about Erik all along?

I won't believe it, Anna thought. She would certainly need to know more than she did now to prove it. Slowly, taking deep, steady breaths, she once more peeked around the corner. Erik and the crewman were still deep in conversation.

The crew member must have just come off duty, Anna thought. *Or be about to begin his shift. Otherwise he wouldn't have the coveralls on.*

As Anna watched, Erik reached into his pocket and handed the young crewman something. Anna bit her lip in frustration. In the next moment Erik grinned and slapped the young man on the shoulder. Anna whipped her head back. It was plain the conversation was about to end, and there was a very good possibility the two men would come straight toward her.

She couldn't let Erik find her lurking on the steps, but she might not make it back up the stairs and out of sight in time. That meant there was only one thing for it. She would have to brazen it out.

Pulling in another deep breath, Anna straightened her back and stepped off the stairway into the B deck corridor—straight into the path of the young crewman. They collided sharply.

"Entschuldigung," the crewman said at once. "Excuse me, fraulein."

"It doesn't matter," Anna responded a little breathlessly.

The crewman reached out to take her arm. Anna bit the inside of her cheek to keep from crying out. Did he know she'd overheard his conversation?

"Did I hurt you? Do you require assistance?" the crewman asked.

"*Nein, danke*," Anna answered. "I was just—" Her voice faltered. *Just what, Anna?* she asked herself. "I thought perhaps . . . a shower . . ."

Oh, God, she thought, *I'm babbling*. But maybe it was better if he thought her idiotic. That way he wouldn't suspect her—if there was anything to be suspicious of, that is.

Oh, God, she thought again. *I can't do this. I'm not like Karl. I don't know how to hide my feelings*. At any moment the crewman might realize how shaken she really was.

And where was Erik? Had he stepped into the shower room to avoid being seen with the crewman? Could he overhear her?

"If you will excuse me," she said, pulling her arm away and spinning on her heel. "My towel—I seem to have forgotten it."

It was all Anna could do not to run up the stairs. But still, her breath was short by the time she reached the top.

I have no choice now, she thought.

She would have to do as she'd promised. It made her skin crawl just to think about it, but now, like the good little spy she was, she had to report what she'd seen and overheard.

With a heart as heavy as the *Hindenburg* was light, Anna set off in search of Karl Mueller.

* * *

She couldn't find him.

Anna prowled through all the public rooms, finally settling in the dining room, where she picked nervously at her breakfast, telling herself that Karl was bound to show up there eventually, but he didn't.

It seemed to Anna as if entire days had gone by, though she knew from looking at her watch that little more than an hour had passed. The rest of the passengers were starting to stir. The dining room was becoming crowded. Surely Karl would come in soon. But still there was no sign of him.

Finally Anna pushed her plate aside. The sight of her uneaten eggs was making her feel nauseated. Besides, it was long past time to face the truth. Since she'd been unable to locate Karl on her own, she could now see only two options: she could ask a member of the crew where Karl was, something they hadn't discussed, which might give away their secret bargain; or she could do nothing and hope that she would encounter him sometime during the day.

If all else failed, Anna could wait until their four o'clock meeting. But how could she keep herself from going crazy until then? she wondered.

"Oh, there you are, Anna. You're up early this morning."

At the sound of Erik's voice, Anna jumped, one startled arm jerking out, striking her plate, and sending it flying off the table. She watched in horror as it landed upside down on top of Erik's perfectly polished shoes.

"I was daydreaming. I didn't hear you," she gasped. "I'm so sorry."

To her astonishment, Erik laughed delightedly. Before she realized what he intended, he leaned down and dropped a kiss on her lips, then bent further to retrieve the plate.

"Just so long as you were daydreaming about me," he said. "Don't go away. I'm going to change my shoes."

He stayed at her side all morning.

He coaxed her into the lounge and plied her with coffee. Lured her into a game of cards, then proceeded to beat her soundly. He finagled a seat at their table for lunch, an act that had so delighted Frau Friedrickson that she'd invited him to join them for dinner also. It would be their last meal on the *Hindenburg*, she reminded them.

"If you are very good, perhaps, Anna will wear her beautiful blue dress once more," she'd teased Erik as they'd strolled along the promenade after lunch.

"In that case," he'd replied, "I will be exemplary."

Anna's stomach had tightened with dismay, but Frau Friedrickson had laughed delightedly.

Erik had then proceeded to be as good as his word. All afternoon he danced attendance on Anna, beginning by persuading Joseph Spah to give an impromptu recital for her.

"You wish me to play another waltz?" he asked, slyly.

"Oh, no," Erik answered. "The waltz is best suited for the night, don't you think?"

That time it was Herr Spah who laughed in delight. Erik had the ability to charm everyone, it seemed.

By the time four o'clock neared, Anna was completely exhausted, her nerves stretched almost to the breaking point, her face sore from smiling. All day long she'd forced her fears to the background, when inside she was seething with confused emotions.

Yesterday she'd wanted to run from Karl Mueller. Last night she'd all but slammed the door in his face. Today all she wanted was to find him.

Finally she pleaded the need for a rest before dinner and escaped to her room. But Anna didn't stay there long, because she had to meet Karl in the reading room. She had to hold up her end of their devil's bargain.

She pulled open her bedroom door and peeked around the corner, feeling like a complete idiot. She didn't even want to think about how she'd feel if Erik caught sight of her.

Once she ascertained that the coast was clear, Anna fled on silent feet down the corridor. Quickly she headed toward the starboard side of the ship, where the lounge and reading room were located. She was grateful for the fact that for once the lounge and the promenade were not crowded.

Halfway along the promenade, she encountered the Ernsts, staring downward somewhat mournfully. The world outside was completely obscured. The *Hindenburg* was sailing through dense clouds. As Anna approached, she saw Otto Ernst reach out to pat his wife's hand consolingly.

"We had so hoped to see the ocean," he explained as Anna reached them. "Your friend Frau Friedrickson said she had seen dolphins."

"It is disappointing," Anna said. "Perhaps later . . ."

But there would be no later, she realized. Tomorrow their journey on the *Hindenburg* would be over.

"Will you excuse me, please?" she said.

"But of course, my dear," Frau Ernst replied at once. "We did not mean to stop you. Come along, Otto. Let's go find a cup of tea."

They moved away from the reading room as Anna continued past them.

Please be here, Karl, she thought, as she passed the partition separating the reading room from the lounge. *Let's get this over with*.

There was no one in the reading room.

No one at the small square writing tables that lined the walls of the reading room, each with a divider in the middle so that it could accommodate two people comfortably, even if one was using a typewriter. No one at the low round tables in the center with their padded chairs. No one leafing through the books on the shelves.

The room was completely deserted.

Anna sank down onto a stool at one of the writing tables, trying to master her desperation. What would she do if Karl didn't come? she wondered. She put her arms on the table and rested her head on them.

Of course Karl would come. Hadn't he been annoyed with her because she'd failed to keep an appointment?

I've got to pull myself together, Anna thought. And when he did arrive, she must not let him see how badly what she'd witnessed had rattled her. That would be as good as admitting that he'd been right about Erik and she'd been wrong.

Anna sat up straight, as she'd always done when faced with one of Kurt's endless lectures.

"Why, Anna!"

At the sound of the familiar voice, Anna struggled to keep her composure. *This can't be happening*, she thought. *It just can't.*

She looked up with a tremulous smile. Erik was lounging in the doorway.

"Hello, Erik," Anna said, her throat as dry as dust.

"What are you doing here?" he asked. "I thought you were resting."

"I couldn't sleep, so I decided to write a letter," Anna said, praying that her excuse sounded genuine. "Then I realized I didn't have any writing paper in my room. So I came in here to get some."

She rose abruptly, clutching several sheets of writing paper that she'd picked up from the table. "I—

I was just about to go back," she stammered. "If you will excuse me? I'll see you at dinner."

"Anna," Erik said. He laid a hand on her arm. Anna started violently. The sheets of writing paper fluttered to the floor. Instantly Anna bent to retrieve them. Erik bent at the same time. Their heads collided.

A bubble of hysterical laughter escaped Anna's lips. Surely this was a horrible dream from which she would wake in the morning. But in the next moment, Erik was laughing too. "What on earth is the matter with you today?" he asked. "I've never known you to be clumsy."

Still laughing, he gathered up the papers and helped her to her feet, keeping one arm around her.

"Your pardon," said a voice from the doorway. And the terrible farce was now complete.

"Ah," Erik said, "good day, Mueller. You will excuse us, won't you? I was just about to escort Fraulein Becker back to her cabin."

Before Anna could say a word, Karl stepped aside and Erik piloted her swiftly out the door.

I tried, Karl, Anna thought. *I really did.*

All the way back to her cabin Anna wondered for the first time if life wouldn't have been easier if she'd simply stayed in Germany.

16

"Well," Frau Friedrickson said as she cut into a thick slice of beef. "What you've told us is absolutely fascinating. I had no idea that working on a zeppelin could be so difficult. Did you, Anna?"

Anna shook her head numbly. As far as she was concerned, dinner was absolute agony. Erik had done little else but speak about the *Hindenburg*. It was plain he knew a very great deal.

I suppose I should be suspicious of this, too, Anna thought. *I should be like Karl: suspicious of everything.*

She speared a bite of the fish she'd chosen but hadn't touched, forced herself to eat it. It felt like sawdust sliding down her throat.

I can't stand this, Anna thought. *I'm no good at hiding my emotions. I want to trust Erik. I want to believe in him. I just don't know how to.* She forced herself to take another bite of fish.

"You must have made many friends among the crew, with all the crossings that you've made," she heard Frau Friedrickson say to Erik.

All of a sudden Anna felt herself perk up. How could she have been so stupid? Once again the solution to her dilemma was plain. They were already speaking about the zeppelin. All Anna had to do was turn the conversation in the direction she wanted it to go.

"Well, I don't know about friends," Erik answered, "but I've certainly struck up some acquaintances."

"The crewmen work hard, don't they?" Anna asked, for the first time joining in the conversation.

"Indeed they do," Erik said, turning toward her.

It just wasn't fair, Anna thought. Now that she was uncertain how she felt about him, she didn't think she'd ever seen Erik look so handsome. The color in his cheeks was high; his green eyes were sparkling.

"And the work doesn't stop when they go off duty," he went on. "Do you know they're not even allowed to bring home presents for their wives and sweethearts?" he asked with the barest suggestion of a wink at Anna.

"But how can that be?" Frau Friedrickson protested before Anna could respond. "On a ship this size, surely there would be room for the men to bring home a few trinkets."

Erik shook his head. "Not according to the Zeppelin Company."

"But why?" Anna asked.

"Because of the extra weight," Erik answered simply. "You saw how carefully our luggage was weighed. If the crew brought things as well . . ." He shrugged.

"But that's so unfair," Anna exclaimed. Erik hesitated for a fraction of an instant, as if trying to make up his mind about something.

"Well," he said leaning forward ever so slightly, his tone turning soft, conspiratorial. "There are ways to get around that restriction. A sympathetic passenger, perhaps, with extra room in his luggage . . ."

He leaned back, let his voice trail off. Anna heard Frau Friedrickson chuckle appreciatively.

Of course, she thought. *Why didn't I see it before?*

It would be like Erik to smuggle something aboard for one of the crewmen. He would enjoy taking a risk others wouldn't take, doing a thing considered forbidden. Hadn't he helped her board the airship in much the same way?

For the first time that day, Anna felt her mood lighten. She had found the thing she'd longed for: an innocent explanation for Erik's encounter with the crewman. Anna was so relieved she felt almost light-headed. The explanation accounted not only for Erik's behavior but also for the crewman's concern about tightened security.

I knew it, she thought. *I knew it was safe to trust Erik. I knew I was right about him and Karl was wrong.*

Without warning, she remembered the feel of Erik's mouth against hers, a thing she'd thought she might have lost forever.

"Good heavens, my dear," Frau Friedrickson exclaimed. "Are you quite well? You've turned as pink as a strawberry."

"I—I just need a little air," Anna stammered. "If you will excuse me."

She pushed away from the table, rose to her feet, and moved swiftly to where one of the promenade windows stood open. She leaned out, drinking in the cool night air. There was never a draft inside the ship, no matter how fast they were moving. Even though her back was to the dining room, she knew the second Erik joined her.

"Are you all right, Anna?"

"I'm fine," she said. She could still feel the relief surging through her body, but she needed to offer some explanation for her unusual behavior. Erik was no fool.

"It's just—you'll think me foolish," she said.

With a gentle pressure on her arm, Erik turned her to face him. "I doubt that very much, Anna."

"All day long I've been worried about tomorrow," she went on, struck by sudden inspiration. "Then all of a sudden, I simply wasn't. I know it doesn't make any sense."

As he'd done the night before, Erik tilted Anna's chin up so that her eyes met his. "Things don't always have to make sense to feel right, Anna."

He's going to kiss me, Anna thought. *Right in front of the entire dining room.* When he lowered his hand, she wasn't sure if she was glad or sorry.

"Now I think you'd better go back and finish your dinner. We have plenty of time to see what else feels right."

For the first time that day, Anna realized she was once more looking forward to something.

"Enjoying yourself, Anna?"

At the sound of the voice behind her in the hallway, Anna spun around and made a quickly smothered exclamation.

It was late at night, a night Anna had spent in the company of Erik and Frau Friedrickson. But the older woman had excused herself early in the evening. Anna was sure that her friend had wanted to make sure that she and Erik had time alone together—time they had used to pleasurable advantage.

But it wasn't Erik who had followed her to her cabin.

Damn you, Karl, Anna thought. It was late, and she was tired. She'd looked forward to a night of pleasant dreams, unlike the one that had awakened her this morning. But Karl had once again surprised her when she wasn't looking.

He *would* turn up now, Anna thought. Now that she didn't want him.

"Did I startle you?" Karl asked when he saw her reaction. "I'm so sorry."

Anna snorted. She leaned back against the door to her cabin, grateful for its support. When it came to dealing with Karl, Anna needed all the backbone she could get.

"You'll have to lie more convincingly than that to stay in the spy business, Karl," she said sharply.

"Don't tell me my business, Anna," Karl said, his voice soft and edgy. "Just answer the question."

"What question?" Anna snapped, beginning to let her irritation get the better of her. *I won't feel guilty*, she thought. *I won't.* And pushed away the tiny voice in the back of her mind, murmuring that she should tell him about Erik.

"What question?" she asked again. "I don't know what you mean, Karl. Stop talking in riddles."

"You know perfectly well what I mean," Karl said, his voice still dangerous. "Are you enjoying yourself with Erik Peterson? Are you enjoying making a fool of me? I thought it was quite clever of you to take him with you to the reading room this afternoon. Such a lovely way to keep your appointment with me without really keeping it."

"But I didn't—" Anna protested, then broke off as Karl took a step toward her.

"And then there's the spectacle you're making of yourself in front of the entire ship. I'm surprised you didn't let him kiss you in front of the whole dining room this evening.

"It's a good thing Anton is dead," Karl went on, his voice brutal. "He would be ashamed of you, Anna. Have you no sense of decency?"

Anna felt a fierce, hot pain shoot straight through her heart. "How dare you?" she said in a tight, furious voice. "You're nothing but a filthy spy. How dare you speak to me of decency? You're the one who wanted me to spend time with Erik in the first place. How I choose to do it is up to me."

Karl's hands curled into fists at his sides. "That's not true and you know it," he said through clenched teeth. "So let me ask you again, Anna. Are you enjoying making a fool out of me?"

"Yes," Anna hissed, letting her anger carry her away completely. "Yes, I'm enjoying it. It's about time you know how it feels to be humiliated. How do you think I felt when I watched you walk away? When I realized all you'd done was lie to me?"

"I—" Karl began, but Anna cut him off.

"I suppose I really should thank you, Karl. You showed me how fickle men could be. Next time I won't be so quick to believe a declaration of love."

Karl took another step forward, his eyes blazing. The expression on his face had Anna fumbling for the door latch.

"Has Peterson said he loves you?"

Anna felt her throat close up.

"Has he told you that he loves you? *Answer me!*"

"I will not," Anna said, amazed to hear her voice come out steady. Her entire body was trembling. "You have no right to question me. You gave that up the day you walked out, Karl, the day you abandoned me without an explanation."

Her fingers found the latch, closed around it. "I'm going in now," she said, sliding the door open behind her. "I'll scream if you try to follow me."

"Anna—"

"Yes, I know, Karl," she answered bitterly. "Tomorrow morning we land in Lakehurst, and you will see that I am sent straight back to Germany. Do me one favor, though, will you? Make sure I don't have to see you before I go."

For the second night in a row she shut the door in his face.

What is going to become of me?

Anna sat on the tiny stool in her cabin, her numb fingers curled around the hairbrush she'd yet to pull through her soft blond hair.

She was trying not to look at her bags, now neatly packed and standing in the corner. At six o'clock the following morning, Anna's desperate flight would be over. The *Hindenburg* would land at the airfield in Lakehurst, New Jersey.

Trying not to think about it, Anna started brushing her hair. It was Ursula who'd taught her this ritual: one hundred strokes just before bedtime. When Anna was little, Ursula had brushed her hair for her. Now Anna always found it soothing. She loved the feel of the bristles prickling ever so slightly against her scalp, then sliding through her tresses, soothing and stimulating all at once. Ursula claimed there was no problem that a good brushing couldn't solve. It cleared the cobwebs from the brain, she'd often told Anna.

Oh, Ursula, Anna thought, as she ran the brush through her hair once more. *How I hope you are right. And how I wish that you were with me.*

Anna had never had such a big problem to solve before, even in the days right after her grandfather's death.

I should have told him.

At the sound of a soft tapping on her door, Anna's hold on the hairbrush slipped. It clattered down onto the dressing table. Anna stared at it, not moving.

What would she do if it was Karl again? She wasn't sure she could face him, but she didn't have a choice. Wearily, she pushed herself to her feet, crossed the cabin, and pulled the door open.

"I hope I'm not disturbing you, my dear. I know it's very late."

"Fr-Frau Friedrickson," Anna stammered. The last person she'd expected. "No, no, of course not."

"May I come in?" Frau Friedrickson asked, surprising Anna yet again.

"Yes, of course," Anna said. "Please do."

Frau Friedrickson bustled into the room, the fringe on the shawl she wore over her dressing gown swaying ever so slightly.

"Oh, you've been brushing your hair," she said,

catching sight of the dressing table. "Such a lovely old-fashioned ritual. I had no idea young women still did that nowadays. I used to brush my daughter's hair when she was little."

Before Anna realized what her friend intended, Frau Friedrickson had picked up the hairbrush. "Do you mind?"

"You want to brush my hair?" Anna asked in astonishment. *Maybe I'm dreaming all of this*, she thought. The visit was growing stranger by the moment.

"You'll humor an old lady, won't you?" Frau Friedrickson asked. "My mother used to say there was no problem a good brushing couldn't solve. And you've one or two problems to work out, haven't you, young Anna?"

Without warning, Anna felt the tears rise in her eyes. Frau Friedrickson sounded so much like Ursula.

"There now," Frau Friedrickson said, crossing back to Anna and piloting her over to the stool. "I've upset you, and that's the last thing I intended. You sit here and let me brush your hair, my dear. And we'll work on those problems together, shall we?"

Unable to think of a word of protest, uncertain if protesting was even what she wanted, Anna sank down onto the stool. A moment later she felt Frau Friedrickson gather her hair together in back and slide the brush through it, just as Ursula had always done. Anna felt her tears spill over.

"There now," Frau Friedrickson said again. "Maybe you should just cry it out, Anna. Sometimes that's the best way, you know."

"I don't know what to do," Anna choked out.

"Well, of course you don't, my dear," Frau Friedrickson answered sensibly. She stroked the brush through Anna's hair once more. "If you knew what to do, you'd have no reason to cry, now, would you?"

As the inescapable logic of her friend's statement sank in, Anna started laughing. *Laughing and crying all at once*, she thought. *If Kurt saw this, he'd lock me up for sure. But at least I wouldn't have to go and live with his colonel.*

"There's something about the way your brain works," she finally managed.

Frau Friedrickson snorted. "I'm scatterbrained, you mean. Yes, I know. My son-in-law tells me so every chance he gets."

Anna sobered at once. "That isn't what I meant," she answered. "I don't think you're scatterbrained at all. In fact, I think it's nothing but a clever disguise."

"Not so clever," Frau Friedrickson retorted. "Not if you can see right through it." But her tone had no sting.

"Now then," Frau Friedrickson continued, "I want you to close your eyes and take a deep breath, then tell me all about whatever is troubling you."

"I need to keep my eyes open," Anna said. And then she told her.

*   *   *

"I can't believe it," Frau Friedrickson said some time later.

She was settled on the stool now, and Anna was sitting on the bunk, her knees pulled up to her chin. By the time she finished her story, her hair had been brushed at least two hundred strokes.

"I just can't believe that nice-looking young blond man is a spy for the Nazis."

"It was hard for me to believe, too, at first," Anna conceded. "But then it all made perfect sense. Besides, he didn't deny it."

Frau Friedrickson sighed and shook her head.

"Now you see why I don't know what to do," Anna continued. "I don't really understand what's happening. I thought that I could trust Karl, that I even loved him once, but he left me. I want to trust Erik, but—"

"But you can't quite discount Karl's suspicions, even though you want to," Frau Friedrickson filled in.

Anna nodded. "I should have told him about Erik and the crewman, even though I'm sure their encounter was perfectly innocent," she admitted miserably. "But he made me so angry that everything else went clean out of my head."

"You certainly do strike sparks off each other," Frau Friedrickson commented.

"It's because we dislike each other so much," Anna said quickly.

"Are you quite certain about that, Anna?" the older woman asked quietly.

Anna felt her pulse stumble. "Of course," she asserted. "What else could it be?"

Frau Friedrickson was silent for a moment. "Every time that young man is in your presence, he has eyes only for you."

"That's because he was watching to make sure I did what he wanted," Anna said at once. "It doesn't mean anything, Frau Friedrickson."

Again the older woman was silent for a moment. "Are you quite certain about that, my dear?" she asked once more.

Anna clasped her hands a little tighter around her knees, remembering the desperate feel of Karl's arms around her. "Don't be afraid of me," he'd all but begged. Because he still loved and wanted her? But he'd walked away and hadn't looked back.

"No," Anna said at last. "I'm not certain. I'm not certain of anything. That's the problem. If only I knew who to believe. Who to trust."

Frau Friedrickson looked surprised for just an instant. "But surely you know one person you can trust, Anna."

"Of course I trust you," Anna said instantly, then was surprised to see Frau Friedrickson shake her head.

"Thank you, my dear, but that isn't what I meant."

Anna felt a headache snaking down between her

eyes. Surely she wasn't going to have to solve yet another mystery.

"Then who—" She stopped short at the expression on the older woman's face.

"Do you really not see? I mean *you*, Anna. Don't you know that you can trust and believe in yourself?"

Anna caught her breath. She'd never thought of it in quite that way before.

"I think I know that," she answered slowly. "Opa always said I had a good head and I shouldn't be afraid to use it."

Frau Friedrickson nodded. "Your grandfather was right, and ordinarily I'd agree with him. But I'm not sure your mind alone can help you solve this problem. I think you must use your heart, too, Anna."

Anna lowered her head to her knees. *But I'm afraid to*, she thought. *Can't you see? I'm so afraid my heart won't do what my head thinks is right.*

Without warning, Erik's voice sounded in her head. *Things don't always have to make sense to feel right, Anna.*

"I'm not suggesting you do anything . . . scatter-brained," Frau Friedrickson continued quietly. With the ghost of a smile, Anna lifted her head.

"And I'm not saying you should ignore your brain entirely. But I am suggesting you turn your mind off for a moment. Listen to your heart speak. It doesn't always say easy things, but I've never known it to lie, have you?"

Anna struggled, then admitted the truth. "No, I haven't."

"I thought as much," Frau Friedrickson said gently. She rose and moved to sit beside Anna on the bunk.

"Here," she said, reaching into the pocket of her dressing gown. "I want you to have something." She pressed something cold into the palm of Anna's hand, then curved Anna's fingers around it tightly.

"My husband gave me this," Frau Friedrickson said. "It was his wedding gift to me. He said it was to remind us both of my spirit. Hugo always said my spirit was the thing that first made him love me. Lord knows it can't have been my looks."

"Frau Friedrickson—" Anna protested.

"Hush now," the older woman said. "Show some respect for your elders and don't interrupt me." But her brown eyes sparkled in the way Anna had come to know so well. "I have thought of my husband, missed him, every single day since his death," Frau Friedrickson said softly. "But I have also been glad that he did not live to see this 'great new Germany' where freedom of spirit is not valued."

She was silent for a moment, then she began to stroke Anna's hair with gentle fingers. "I think you have a brave spirit and a brave heart, Anna Becker. Don't throw your greatest gifts away. Without a great heart, you cannot have a great mind." Frau Friedrickson rose to her feet.

Speechless, Anna stared up at her.

"It would make me very happy if you would wear my gift tomorrow when we land at Lakehurst," Frau Friedrickson said quietly. She leaned down and kissed Anna on the forehead. "And now I will say good night, my dear. Sleep well, Anna." She crossed the room and opened the door, then slid it silently closed behind her.

Only then did Anna open her hand, gasping in surprise at what she saw: in her palm was an exquisite brooch shaped like a bird in flight.

When Anna turned it so that the stones caught the light, she felt her breath halt in her throat.

The heart of each stone blazed with a blue she knew all too well. The same color as Karl's eyes.

Anna managed to fumble her writing table open and set the brooch on it before the first sob burst from her. Alone in her cabin, on the last night of her journey, she did the thing she'd not done once since her grandfather's death: she cried herself to sleep, her mind open at last to the secrets her heart had always told her.

Anna awoke the next morning heavy-hearted. Acknowledging the truth about the past hadn't made her prospects for the future any brighter. There was absolutely no doubt in her mind about what would happen next: as soon as they landed, Karl would take whatever steps were necessary to make certain Anna was sent back to Germany.

But when Anna had risen and dressed once more in her pale gray dress, she checked her watch and discovered it was eight A.M., two full hours after they were supposed to have landed in Lakehurst, New Jersey. She pinned Frau Friedrickson's brooch to the front of her dress, then hurried from her cabin. On the landing by the stairs, she encountered the stewardess, Frau Imhof.

"Ah, fraulein," the other woman said before Anna had even had time to address her. "No doubt you are wondering why we have not landed."

"It's true," Anna admitted. "I was."

"The strong headwinds we encountered during our crossing have delayed us," Frau Imhof answered. "I am not certain of our exact arrival time at Lakehurst, but I can tell you it will be many hours from now. We are not likely to reach the landing field until late afternoon at least."

"Thank you," Anna said. As she turned away, she heard the stewardess offer her explanation to yet another passenger.

Many hours, Anna thought. Would they be hours of reprieve or of further torture? How would she fill her time until the *Hindenburg* landed?

One thing she knew for certain: she could not go back to her cabin. She was sure the smallness of it, once so comforting, would now serve only to remind her of how small her life would soon become.

Feet dragging on the *Hindenburg*'s lush carpets, Anna made her way to the dining room. She forced herself to eat a hearty breakfast, half expecting to see Frau Friedrickson at any moment. But the older woman never joined her.

All morning long the zeppelin floated through a thick gray mist. Even gazing out the windows did not break the monotony.

Anna wandered up and down the dining room promenade, then switched sides and paced along the reading room and lounge. For a while, determined to distract herself, she tried counting the number of times she walked each length. She gave up when she reached a hundred.

I am pacing like a caged animal, she thought, as she let her footsteps lead her once more toward the dining room. The only good thing about the activity was that it had helped to pass the morning and had kept her from having to make conversation with other passengers. For once, Anna didn't feel like company.

Anna touched Frau Friedrickson's brooch, pinned to the front of her dress. The pin with its beautiful blue stones was Anna's only spot of color. But even this token failed to lift her spirits. It was too clear a reminder of her own fear, of all her heart now urged her to do but her mind could not find the courage to accomplish.

I couldn't follow my heart, even if I found the courage, Anna thought morosely. She had seen neither Erik nor Karl all morning.

"You seem worried, my dear. Won't you sit down and join us?"

Surprised, Anna turned her head. The Ernsts were sitting at a table for two in the dining room. As usual, they were drinking tea. Also as usual, the sight of them produced a rush of emotion in Anna.

Someday, I want to grow old with someone, just as these two have grown old together, she thought.

"My mood is not very good, I'm afraid," she said, with an attempt at a smile.

"Never mind about that," Frau Ernst said at once. "A good cup of tea is just what you need."

Her husband got up to fetch a chair. Anna joined them.

"This waiting is so difficult, isn't it?" Frau Ernst said sympathetically, when Anna was settled. "And the mist is so boring, not to mention disappointing! I had hoped to see so many wonderful things on this trip . . . but no matter. Perhaps the weather will be better on our return journey."

"Look, Else!" her husband exclaimed suddenly. "It is clearing!"

"Oh, Otto, you're just trying to cheer me up," his wife scolded.

"Actually, I think Herr Ernst is right," Anna said. "Shall we go and see?"

Together the three of them moved to the windows. Within seconds, the promenade railing was crowded.

"Look!" Frau Ernst cried suddenly. "I can see something."

A wash of sunlight poured through the windows as the mists abruptly parted.

"We're over land!" Frau Ernst cried excitedly. "Over a city. Where are we, does anyone know?"

Farther down the promenade, a man's voice said, "That is Boston."

The airship was so low that Anna could see the

roofs of the buildings, but it was difficult to see much of the city because the *Hindenburg* continued to drift in and out of fog. What she could see, however, went a long way toward reviving her downcast spirits.

I did it, Anna thought.

She had taken her life in her hands and flown all the way to America. She knew her first sight of it was one she would remember through all the long, dark years that lay ahead for her in Germany.

She turned to the Ernsts. "Thank you," she said impulsively.

"Think nothing of it, my dear," Otto Ernst said. "We are always happy to produce a city when you want one. Now come and have some lunch."

Laughing, she walked with them to the dining room.

The *Hindenburg* reached New York in the late afternoon. To Anna, it seemed that the whole airship buzzed with the excitement of it. Even veteran travelers like Frau Friedrickson turned out to see the great city come into view.

The sights and sounds were electrifying. Factory whistles and car horns sounded as the *Hindenburg* sailed overhead. In a blinding burst of light, the sun came out just as the airship reached the Empire State Building. The sight of the tall building made Anna catch her breath, even as she joined her fellow passengers in leaning out the promenade windows to wave her handkerchief at the people standing on its observation deck.

The *Hindenburg* sailed so close that Anna could almost count the sightseers, see the winks of light from the camera lenses as photographers swiveled them upward, preparing to take a picture of the great airship.

A few moments later Anna saw the Statue of Liberty standing like a tiny porcelain figure in the harbor. But she could also see the bank of dark clouds that rose behind it. The farther the ship got from New York, the thicker and darker the clouds became. By the time the *Hindenburg* had made the short trip to southern New Jersey and Lakehurst, the wind was gusting and rain was falling.

"The captain will never be able to land in this," Frau Friedrickson predicted. "The wind is too strong."

And sure enough, she was proved right a moment later. The *Hindenburg* circled the airfield once. Through the rain, Anna could see the huge, empty hangar. Then the airship continued on, heading toward New Jersey's southern coast.

Anna felt her high spirits abruptly desert her. Now that she had actually seen the airfield, the reality of her situation felt oppressively close. She leaned her head against the promenade window.

What would he be like? she wondered. This person Kurt had asked to retrieve her like a lost parcel, one he didn't really want but was unwilling to give up because it might yet have some value.

Stop it, now, she told herself disgustedly. *You're just feeling sorry for yourself. That will never help you. You made your bid for freedom and you failed. The least you can do is to face it squarely. Make Opa proud of you.*

She tried not to think of what would make Opa proudest of all. That she would seek out Karl Mueller and tell him the truth.

All of a sudden Anna found it impossible to be still. Even if it meant pacing the promenades another hundred times, she had to keep moving. It was the only way she could keep from dwelling on her painful thoughts.

"Will you excuse me, please?" she asked Frau Friedrickson.

"Of course, Anna," her friend answered. "I'll look for you when we disembark. Don't worry. I don't think it will be too much longer."

Don't worry, Anna thought as she prowled the ship, disconsolately. As she had that morning, she lost all track of time. But all around her, she could see the signs of their imminent arrival.

Stewards bustled to and fro. The hallways that led to the cabins were filled with bedding and laundry. Frau Imhof helped the boy Anna had first seen at the customs check search for a lost shoe, laughing when they triumphantly unearthed it from beneath a pile of sheets.

Everyone was ready, even eagerly awaiting, the arrival at Lakehurst. Everyone, it seemed, but Anna. She climbed up and down between A deck and B, hardly noticing where she was going, propelled by her desire to keep moving.

Maybe sooner or later I'll turn in the right direction, she thought.

"Hello, Anna."

Startled, Anna skidded to a stop. Without realizing it, her feet had carried her to the reading room. It was long after four o'clock, but Karl was there. Had he been there all this time, waiting?

"I was just walking," Anna said, then could have kicked herself. Here at last was her opportunity. There was so much she should say, so much she wished to say, and so little time in which to do it. Yet here she was, sounding like an idiot.

"Karl," she said in a low voice, "may I speak with you?"

Surprise showed in Karl's face before he could conceal it. Looking up at him, Anna was surprised herself, to see how tired he looked. His skin was pale and waxy. His deep blue eyes had dark smudges under them.

"But of course you may, Anna." Karl glanced back over his shoulder into the reading room. Several passengers had settled down to write last-minute letters. "But not here, I think," he said.

His gaze flicked to a bench at the very end of the promenade, on the other side of the reading room railing. It would put them as far away as possible

172

from the passengers in the reading room. At Karl's gesture, Anna moved toward the bench, trying not to remember that she'd been there last night, with Erik.

She sat down and folded her hands tightly in her lap. "Won't you sit down, Karl?" she invited. "I'll get a crick in my neck if I have to keep staring up at you."

The truth was, Anna was sure she'd lose her courage with him towering over her. Karl hesitated a moment, then did as she asked. But Anna noticed he was careful to sit so that he did not touch her. Her heart wrenched painfully inside her chest.

Just say it, she told herself. *Get it over.*

"I want to apologize for what I said last night," she said in a low voice. "I spoke in anger. I'm sure Opa would not have wanted us to part that way, Karl."

Though they did not touch, Anna was close enough to feel the surprise ripple through Karl's body. His head swung toward her as if pulled by a string.

"And you? What do you want, Anna?"

Anna took a deep breath and let her heart speak. "I do not wish it either," she admitted softly. "After all that we have been to each other, I do not want us to part in anger."

It seemed to Anna that Karl held his breath. She fell silent for a moment. When he did not speak, she continued in a rush. "I'm sorry, Karl. Sorry for what has happened between us. I never meant to make you hate me so much."

She felt rather than heard Karl expel his pent-up breath, though he still did not touch her.

"But you are wrong," he said. His voice was strained as he struggled to keep it low and steady.

"I do not hate you. I love you, Anna. I have always loved you. I never stopped, not even for a moment."

Stars exploded in front of Anna's eyes. She felt as if she'd taken a hard blow to the stomach.

"Then *why?*" she burst out. "Why did you go?"

"Because I had no choice, Anna. It was the only way I knew to keep you safe, to protect you."

"Protect me from what?" she demanded.

For the first time, Karl reached for her, taking her hand in his. His fingers were like ice. "From a fate I could not foresee. There have been threats against the *Hindenburg*, Anna. Threats to destroy the zeppelins aren't really anything new. There have always been such things, particularly since the airships started displaying the swastikas. Usually we dismiss such threats as the ravings of fanatics."

"But not this time," Anna said.

"No," Karl answered. "This time the situation seemed different, more possible, more real. Late last season detailed plans of the airship were found in the apartment of a man who'd made frequent crossings. Someone tipped him off, and he escaped. After that, we decided to keep an eye on anyone making frequent crossings."

Anna felt a cold chill sweep over her. "Like Erik Peterson."

Karl nodded. "Yes, like Peterson. Watching him is just a precaution, Anna. We do not know for sure that he plans any mischief."

Anna could feel her mind struggling to make sense of something. Abruptly, it focused on a single word. "We?" she said.

For the first time since they'd sat down, Karl looked directly at her. "I work for the Zeppelin Company," he said quietly. "For Herr Eckener, himself. You must know that he is not a Nazi."

All Germany knows that, Anna thought. The Zeppelin Company director, some said the greatest airship captain of them all, had been declared a nonperson for his scathing comments on the Nazi party. He was not allowed to be interviewed, nor could his photograph be printed anywhere in the country.

"You are not a Nazi spy?" she said.

"I suppose it is fair to say I am a spy of sorts," Karl answered, "but not for the Nazis, for the Zeppelin Company. Because the company wanted to keep its investigation of the recent threats as quiet as possible, I could tell no one about my work, not even you and Anton. It had to be conducted in secrecy.

"Leaving Frankfurt, knowing you would think I had abandoned you, was the hardest thing I have ever done, Anna. The most I could do, when I felt the danger was real, was to write to Anton to warn him of the danger."

Anna's body tingled with shock. "You wrote to my grandfather?" she asked, astonished.

Karl looked surprised. "But I thought you knew. I sent him a telegram, telling him to cancel your trip, that it wasn't safe to make the crossing. I would have been fired if the company learned what I had done. But I had to try to keep you and your grandfather safe."

"Safe?" Anna cried out. She thought her heart would burst within her. She understood now. Too much. Too late. "You did not keep him safe. It was your telegram that killed him!"

19

Karl shot to his feet. "What are you talking about, Anna? What are you saying?"

"The day my grandfather died, he received a telegram," Anna answered. "I never saw it. He read it once, then burned it."

Her words were choked off as she once more saw her grandfather's tortured face. "He turned to me, Karl," she continued in a low voice. "He called to me. Just once, he said my name. Then he collapsed. He died later that night."

"My God," Karl whispered, his face ashen. "I did not know. Anna, you must believe me."

"He tried to tell me something right before he died." Anna spoke slowly as if she were reciting a lesson.

"He pulled my ticket from his bedside drawer. I thought he was telling me to *make* the crossing—to go without him and never come back to Germany. He knew what my life would be like without him, if I stayed. He knew what Kurt would plan for me."

Anna raised her eyes to Karl's and found her torture mirrored there.

"But he wasn't, was he? He was trying to warn me not to make the trip. He knew it wasn't safe. He knew because you'd told him, but he never told me. Dear God, Karl, I've been such a fool. What is going to become of me, of us all?"

Karl drew her up into the shelter of his arms. "I do not know, Anna," he said honestly. "The truth is, we don't even know if there really is a danger. We have never known it for certain. All we can do is watch and try to be ready. So far, Peterson has done nothing unusual that I can discover. All may yet be well."

No, Anna thought. She saw the truth now. Finally her brain was functioning.

It was Erik who'd first suggested that Karl was a Nazi spy. Erik who'd recognized Anna's strong feelings for Karl, played on them, led her to mistrust him. And it was Erik who'd told the story of the hard lives of the zeppelin crew members.

To cover his back, Anna thought, because he knew she'd been watching him?

And she had believed it—all of it. Because she'd been afraid to listen to her heart. She'd let her mind stifle her instincts.

It will never be all right, she thought. *It can't be. Merciful heavens, what have I done?*

She pushed free of Karl's arms, knowing she could never tell him about Erik while he was holding her.

"I saw him talking to one of the zeppelin crew," she gasped out. "I recognized the coveralls the crewman was wearing."

"Wait, Anna. Slow down. What are you saying?" Karl demanded.

"I saw Erik Peterson," Anna repeated. "I saw him give something to one of the crew."

"When?" Karl said, seizing her by the elbows.

"Yesterday morning."

Karl's eyes blazed out, filled with pain and fury.

"Yesterday morning," he echoed. "And you did not tell me."

"I tried," Anna said desperately. "I couldn't find you, Karl. I didn't know what to do. I didn't know if I should ask for you or not. You never told me why I was to watch Erik. You never explained the situation. All you did was threaten and bully."

"You made sure you couldn't tell me," Karl countered, his voice low and tight. "You made sure Peterson would be safe by bringing him with you to the reading room. Do you love him so much, then?"

"Of course I don't, you idiot," Anna all but shouted. "I love you."

Karl stared at her, eyes wide with surprise. Anna stared right back, straight into them. Then, slowly, in the very backs of Karl's blue eyes, Anna thought she saw the thing she'd once believed was gone for-ever: hope.

"I love you, Karl," she said, the voice straight from her heart. "Believe me, I tried hard not to. I even thought I'd managed it, but only with my head. My heart always knew the truth. It knew I had never stopped loving you."

"Anna—"

"Oh, stop talking!" Anna said, torn between laughter and tears. "Conversation only gets us into trouble."

Karl put his mouth down over hers.

Anna knew she would remember this kiss for the rest of her life. The bitter and the sweet entwined together. Hopes and fears inextricably mixed. Like their lives had been. Pain and laughter.

"Are we going to die, Karl?" she whispered when the kiss was over.

"Dear God," Karl said. "Not if I can help it. Not now that I've found you again, Anna. But I've got to go. I've got to find out what Erik did, to try to stop him. Would you recognize the crewman if you saw him again?"

"I think so," Anna said.

"Then perhaps there is still time—"

"There is no time, Mueller," said a quiet voice behind them. "You are too late. Look around you. We are landing."

20

"No," Anna gasped.

Erik stood just behind them, blocking their access to the rest of the ship.

"I'm afraid the answer is yes. Look around you," he repeated.

Anna looked out of the promenade window and saw the airfield just below her. While she and Karl had been wrapped up in each other, the *Hindenburg* had returned to Lakehurst and was being maneuvered into landing position. Anna could see mooring ropes, dangling down from the bow.

"Peterson," Karl growled, "what have you done?"

"What had to be done," Erik answered, his face flushed with color, his green eyes shining. "This symbol of the Third Reich must be destroyed. The world must be shown that the Nazis are not invincible. That they can be stopped."

"And the passengers, the crew?" Karl asked. "They are to be sacrificed, is that it?"

The color in Erik's cheeks deepened. He glanced toward Anna, but now she could see that his eyes were tortured.

"It had to be done," he whispered. "Too many people have disappeared. Who knows when it will end? You must understand. I had no choice. I had to try to stop it."

"There is *always* a choice, Erik," Anna protested.

Erik shook his head, his expression anguished. "Only between two great evils," he answered. "You should understand how difficult that kind of choice is. You cannot think I wished to do this, Anna."

"Then stop before it is too late," Anna said. "Don't do this, Erik!"

"But I have told you, Anna," Erik said. "It is already too late."

"I don't believe that," Anna said.

Karl made a sudden move. "I'm going to the captain."

"No!" Erik cried. "No, you must not."

With a great shout, he flung himself upon Karl. Anna pressed herself against the seat, watching in horror as the two men grappled. People in the reading room and all along the promenade turned to see what was causing the commotion.

I must do something, Anna thought. *I must help Karl.*

But she could see no way to do it. She could not get past the two combatants to reach the captain. And the two men were locked too close together for her to interfere with them directly. If she tried to wound Erik, she might accidentally injure Karl instead. Besides, she had no weapon.

"Help me," she cried out in desperation. "Somebody call the captain!"

At the sound of her voice, Erik's hold loosened for just a second. Karl pulled away, then lunged toward him. But Erik was too quick. He sidestepped, striking Karl on the back of the neck, using his own momentum against him. Karl tumbled to the floor and did not get up.

"No," Anna cried out. "No!"

She would have flung herself down beside Karl, but Erik caught her. Anna struggled, flailing wildly.

"Help me," she called out once more.

"I am the only one who can help you now," Erik panted. "Stop fighting me, Anna."

"What's going on here?" a voice barked. Anna opened her mouth to speak. At that moment Erik lifted his head as if listening for something. The words Anna would have spoken died in her throat. A great unnatural stillness seemed to settle over her, over the whole airship. Even the *Hindenburg*'s great engines were silent. Anna held her breath.

Then, in the quiet, she heard a soft pop, like a bottle being opened. Erik's green eyes looked down to fasten upon hers.

"*Es ist das Ende.* It is the end, Anna."

Without warning, the whole airship trembled. Erik gave a low groan—of joy or anguish, Anna couldn't tell which.

"In the name of God, Erik," she whispered, "what have you done?"

In the next instant she and Erik were hurled to the floor as the *Hindenburg* tilted backward. Anna's ears were filled with a roar of sound: the crash of furniture as it toppled over and slid along the deck, the jangling of the overturned piano, the screams of her fellow passengers.

She caught a glimpse of Karl, still unconscious, crushed against the end of the promenade.

I must get to him, Anna thought. *And then I must find Frau Friedrickson.*

But she could do neither. She couldn't even get to her feet. Now the airship rolled from side to side. With each pitch, Anna heard the screams of the passengers increase. Like her, they could not get their bearings. Anna felt her strength, her hope, begin to fade. *There is no way out of this,* she thought.

And then she felt the heat sweep over her.

Never in her life had Anna imagined such heat. This was no contained fire meant to warm her on a winter's night. This was a fire straight from the mouth of hell, a roaring inferno.

Anna felt the heat blast against her face, until she thought her skin would split open and peel back from the intensity of it. Burning pieces of the *Hin-*

denburg's skin fluttered down around her like flaming birds. Instinctively, Anna tried to pound them out, even though her desperate brain screamed that it was futile.

I am going to die here, she thought. *Erik was right. This is the end.*

She tried to crawl toward Karl, but Erik still held her. To her astonishment, he managed to rise and yank her to her feet.

"This way. We must get to the front of the ship, Anna."

"No," Anna screamed desperately. She tried to pull back, but Erik had too tight a hold on her. "Karl!"

"Do not be a fool," Erik gasped. "You cannot save him."

"No," Anna tried to scream again. But the very air choked her. It was so hot she felt it burn its way down into her lungs.

I can't stand much more of this, she thought. Soon it wouldn't make a bit of difference where she was on the ship. Surely in another minute this would all be over.

Halfway down the promenade Erik stopped. As if she had all the time in the world, Anna looked down out of the window.

The ground crew members were so close she could almost read their facial expressions. The ground moved toward her so quickly that the sight of it made Anna dizzy.

With a great cry, Erik lifted one leg and sent it crashing through the window directly in front of them.

"Now!" he shouted.

Before Anna realized what he intended, he grasped her by both arms and swung her body out into space, his eyes looking past her, as if gauging the distance to the ground below her.

Then, for one final moment, those green eyes that had reminded her so much of life itself, gazed straight into hers.

"You are the only thing that I regret," he said.

He released her arms and stepped back into the fire.

21

Anna plummeted downward. She heard a wild crackling in the air around her, twisted her head from side to side, and realized that her hair had caught fire. In the next moment she smelled it, rank in her nostrils. And worse than that, the smell of burning flesh. Hers? Or someone else's?

Then, with a force that knocked the air from her aching lungs, Anna landed on the sand of the landing field, flat on her back. Her ears rang with the force of her fall. She felt as though every bone in her body must surely be broken. But she forced herself to roll from side to side, pressing her head into the soft, wet sand of the airfield, desperately trying to put out her flaming hair.

Then, spent, she lay still for a moment, gasping

for breath. And saw the bulk of the airship burning across the night sky like a great fireworks display directly above her.

The tail of the *Hindenburg* was now completely on the ground. Flames raced along the top of the airship, spouted from the front end like a geyser. Burning aluminum fell like fiery rain.

Anna knew she should get up, get out of the way. But she couldn't move. All her strength had left her. All she could do was lie on the ground, staring up at the letters that still spelled out the name of the great zeppelin, invincible pride of the invincible Third Reich. Then, as she watched, the fire took the name, too, spreading to devour the first part, "Hinden."

For a moment it seemed to Anna as if, against all odds, the rest of the name would survive. In the time it took Anna to pull in one aching breath, absolutely nothing happened.

Then fire mushroomed out from the very center of the panel containing the rest of the name, reaching with hungry fingers to the flames on either side of it. "Burg" vanished, consumed in an instant. Flaming pieces of the outer skin streaked down around Anna.

There was nothing that could save the airship. Absolutely nothing.

She realized now what her eyes had seen but her heart hadn't wanted to acknowledge.

There were still people on board the airship, and

now they were jumping. A member of the crew dangled from the nose, high in the air, then lost his grip and hurtled downward. Anna could see his legs pump and flail.

It's too high, she thought. *He'll never survive the fall.*

In the next instant she was astonished to see the gangways being lowered to the ground, exactly as if the ship were making a normal landing. A woman staggered down them. A moment later Anna saw two more people descend, arm in arm.

"Run, run! Get out of the way!" Anna heard voices shouting. For the first time, she realized there were people all around her—passengers and crew from the *Hindenburg*, the landing crew from New Jersey, all staggering through the fiery rain the night had become, desperate to find a place of safety.

I have to move, Anna thought. *I can't stay here.* She tried to get up, but her legs refused to hold her, and she fell heavily to her hands and knees. Above her, at her back, she could feel the fierce heat of the flames as the airship sank lower and lower.

Move, move, move! she thought.

If she wasn't fast enough, she would die after all. The burning ship would fall on top of her.

Sobbing now, Anna crawled forward, then cried out in pain and fear as a huge piece of burning aluminum fell directly in front of her.

She stopped, covering her head with her arms and hands. There was no way to predict where the burning debris would fall, no way to choose which direction to go to avoid it.

I can't stop, she thought. *I can't stay here. I've got to move faster*. Once more she staggered to her feet. This time her legs supported her.

"Lady," she heard a voice cry. "Lady, come this way."

In the next instant, there were arms around her. Anna felt herself being pulled forward. She stumbled, felt herself being jerked upright. Burning debris fell like sheets of hail.

"Keep moving," the voice shouted. "We've got to get clear of the ship."

But I can't leave it yet, Anna's weary, disoriented mind responded. *I'm missing something. Something I must go back for. Something important. Something I cannot live without.*

But what was it?

"Navy men, stand fast!" Anna heard a great voice bellow.

"Take her," the voice closest to Anna commanded. She felt herself being thrust forward into a second pair of arms. Hardly knowing what she did, Anna turned to watch her unknown rescuer sprint back toward the airship.

Her whole mind exploded.

She knew what she'd left behind now. The most precious thing to her in the whole world. The thing that made her life worth living.

She had left her love behind. No matter that she hadn't had a choice.

"No," she whispered through her burned, parched throat. "No, I must go back." And felt the arms around her tighten.

"You cannot go back, fraulein. You must stay here, where it is safe."

"You don't understand, I must go back! I must go back!" Anna shouted.

The strong arms pulled her from the airfield then, toward the building where they were already tending to the survivors. As long as her legs would hold her, as long as her mind would function, Anna struggled.

Even after she knew it was futile, after the *Hindenburg* had burned away to nothing but a shell of twisted smoking metal.

After Anna's voice grew painful, hoarse, and then gave out altogether. After they'd taken her to the airfield hospital, where the doctors had bandaged her badly blistered hands, treated the burns on her scalp and forehead, tended wounds Anna hadn't even known she had.

After they'd made her lie down, telling her there was no more that she could do, that she must save her strength, that she must rest.

Even then, Anna's lips still moved, repeating the same thing, over and over: "I must go back. I must go back."

Back for the true love she'd never wished to leave behind. Back for Karl Mueller.

22

He was dying, and there was nothing she could do.

Anna sat by Karl's bedside, her bandaged hands resting useless in her lap. For two long days she had watched him suffer, watched him fight, struggling to win his battle against death.

But the doctors had told her the truth. It was astonishing that Karl had survived at all, pulled from the airship by members of the desperate ground crew. When they dragged him, still unconscious, from the fiery wreckage, Karl's blackened skin had stuck to their hands, his burns were so severe.

His clothes had been burned away before his rescuers had even reached him. There was not a place on Karl's body the fire hadn't touched. He could not survive, no matter how strong his will.

And so Anna had done the only thing she could do, the thing she'd done for her grandfather: she'd sat by his bedside through the long hours, silently praying for a miracle.

But even as she prayed, Anna was in the grip of a feeling of guilt so strong that it threatened to overwhelm her. If Karl died, it would be her fault, just as all the deaths on the great airship had been her fault.

Because, in the end, she had used neither her mind nor her heart. She had not warned Karl in time because she'd let her hurt pride blind her.

Now thirty-six people lay dead or dying, victims of the fire. Anna was sure the number would stay etched into her mind forever. The victims included twenty-two members of the *Hindenburg*'s crew; one member of the Lakehurst ground crew who hadn't had Anna's good fortune and had lost his life as the burning zeppelin literally fell from the skies and landed on top of him; and thirteen passengers, Herr Ernst and Frau Friedrickson among them. Frau Friedrickson had died before the airship touched the ground, Anna had been told. But word of Herr Ernst's death had come just that morning. It was the Ernsts whom Anna had seen staggering down the gangway, still together, even in those last desperate moments.

But Else Ernst would be alone from now on, just as Anna would.

So many lives lost, Anna thought. *And all are on my head. My conscience.* She tried not to think at all about

Erik Peterson. He, too, was among the dead. But his final act had meant her salvation.

"Anna . . ."

At the whisper of sound from the bed, Anna started. Karl's eyes were open, their alpine-lake blue clouded with pain but fixed on her. She placed one bandaged hand beside his head, wishing with all her heart that she could touch him, but she dared not; his injuries were too severe and her bandaged hands too clumsy.

"Anna," Karl whispered again.

Anna leaned down. "It's all right. I am here, Karl," she answered.

"The ship," Karl said.

Anna felt her breath twist like a knife inside her chest. "Gone, Karl," she answered. "But Captain Pruss is still alive, and so are most of the passengers."

Karl tried to frame a word, failed, then tried again.

"Peterson," he finally gasped out.

Anna felt the knife twist deeper, felt her heart bleeding. She shook her head, watching as Karl closed his eyes briefly.

"I should not . . . be glad," he said slowly, as he opened them again. "But he should not survive." He pulled in a shuddering breath. "Not when we have lost so many others."

He closed his eyes again. Anna could see him struggle for breath. Talking to her was taking all his energy.

"You should not talk so much, Karl," she murmured urgently. "You should rest and save your strength."

Once again, Karl opened his beautiful eyes. This time, Anna was astonished to see that the pain had vanished. They were clear and shining.

"I want . . ." Karl said. Again he paused to take a breath. "I do not want to die. I want to *live*, Anna."

A strange sound began to rise in Anna's head.

"You will live," she answered. "The doctors tell me you are getting better. We will be together, Karl. Just as we should be. Just as Opa always wanted. I can't wait to see the look on Kurt's face when we tell him, can you?"

Karl's lips curved into a smile. Unable to refrain from touching him any longer, Anna laid her fingertips against the bandages wrapped around his forehead.

"I love you. I have always loved you, Anna."

"And I love you," she answered honestly. Then she repeated his own words back to him. "I never stopped, not even for a moment."

Anna felt the sound grow until it was the only thing she could hear, resonating throughout her entire body. Only this time, Anna knew it for what it was: the sound of own heart breaking.

Karl's eyes smiled up into hers, the expression in them blinding. Then, slowly, as if he were a small child falling asleep during a bedtime story, his burned eyelids dropped over them. They fluttered once, as if he wished to open them again but lacked the strength. Then he became motionless.

Anna watched him take one breath. Then two. She found herself breathing to the same rhythm. Five more times she breathed in and out with the silent man on the bed. On the sixth time, Karl's breath came out, then stopped.

Anna felt the salt tears scald the burns on her own cheeks.

She had lost the two people she loved most in the world. Now she had no one left.

Erik was right. This was the end.

23

Days later, Anna stood in a huge warehouse on the New York docks, looking at the coffins of the dead. Knowing that it was now just a matter of hours before she must return to Germany.

In fact, it was hard to imagine she wasn't there now. The coffins were draped with German flags. Swastika banners hung above them. Passing mourners gave stiff-armed salutes, particularly to the coffin of the charismatic airship pioneer, Captain Ernst Lehmann. He had succumbed to his wounds, while the more seriously injured Captain Pruss had not.

Anna had heard it whispered that Captain Lehmann had simply given up, that his spirit had been broken.

I should know how that feels, Anna thought. But the

truth was that she felt nothing. Since Karl's death Anna had been enveloped in a dense gray cloud like the one that had surrounded the *Hindenburg* through much of the last part of its voyage to America.

The airship had burst through to sunshine, Anna remembered. But she didn't think she would ever do so. In fact, she hoped she would not. It was so much safer to feel nothing.

Because if Anna once acknowledged what was swirling deep inside her heart, she was sure her feelings would rise up to choke her.

They shouldn't be here, she thought as she stared at the coffins. *None of them.* But they were, and it was all her fault. She'd had the power to prevent all this death and disaster, but she hadn't used it. She had done nothing.

Anna felt the cocoon of gray mist slip and a spurt of fear shoot through her as she watched a group of German officials move along the line of coffins. Both American and German authorities were seeking the cause of the disaster. The investigation had begun the day Karl died, two days after the explosion.

If the authorities suspected sabotage, what would she do? Anna wondered. Regardless of what they suspected, should she go to them? Didn't she owe it to Karl and the others to tell the truth?

"You do not wish to pay your respects, fraulein?"

At the sound of a voice beside her elbow Anna almost jumped. At the last moment she caught herself. She knew without turning who the voice belonged to: Herr Heiss, the man her brother had chosen to make sure she was returned to Germany.

What does it matter what I wish? Anna almost asked. But once again, she caught herself. Herr Heiss already had enough power over her; there was no sense in giving him even more. In the grim, gray days following Karl's death, only the sight of Herr Heiss had had the power to pierce Anna's defenses.

She'd tried telling herself that she was being unfair to him. That it wasn't his fault she'd hated him on sight. It was also not his fault that his thin face and long pale hands reminded her of a rodent's.

But it hadn't done any good. Herr Heiss was the symbol of everything from which Anna had tried to escape. He was the agent of the fate she could no longer avoid, the life her brother had chosen for her.

At times Anna had considered simply running away, but much as she wished to avoid the life she knew was waiting for her in Germany, she hadn't been able to bring herself to flee. The fire, which had taken so much from her, now seemed to take her will to fight.

The deaths on the *Hindenburg* felt too much like her fault. Abandoning the dead was too much like betrayal.

And Anna's inability to act in her own defense had only increased her dislike of the man her brother had sent for her.

Herr Heiss peered at her now through wire-rimmed glasses that always seemed about to slide down his nose. "I asked you a question, Fraulein Becker," he said. "Did you not hear me?"

Suddenly Anna had had enough. It wasn't true that she felt nothing: the sight of this man filled her with such loathing that she could hardly bring herself to speak.

"Of course I heard you, Herr Heiss," she answered, her voice strangled. "But you would not wish me to make a spectacle of myself, surely. It was I, not you, who traveled on the *Hindenburg*. It was I who survived its devastation. You must let me make my farewells in my own time. I am the one with friends in those coffins."

Herr Heiss's narrow faced flushed at her answer. "You would do well to remember, Fraulein Becker," he said in a low voice, "that you have caused your own suffering. If you had stayed in Germany as your brother wished, you would not now have any reason to mourn."

Oh, yes, Anna thought. *I can still feel something: I can hate.* She hated this man who would take everything from her, even her grief.

You are smarter than he is, she told herself. *Don't let him provoke you. Use your head, Anna.*

"Even my brother sent condolences on the death of Karl Mueller," she answered. "He was an old friend of the family. And I am sure the dead suffered much more than I do, Herr Heiss. Now, if you will excuse me . . ."

"Do not forget, fraulein," he hissed as she moved away. "The *Europa* sails tomorrow."

This time, Anna didn't answer. *As if I could forget,* she thought, as she took her place in the line of mourners passing in front of the coffins.

The bodies of the dead would make their journey home to Germany on the steamship *Hamburg*. The living would travel on the *Europa*. Anna would be home by the end of the month. Her bid for freedom would be over.

Slowly she walked along the row of wooden coffins until she reached Frau Friedrickson's. With surprise, Anna saw that Karl's sat beside it. As they did in her heart, the two people Anna had loved most on the *Hindenburg* lay beside each other in death.

Anna halted. Her fingers went instinctively to the brooch she still wore, the only possession she had that had survived the fire.

Anna felt her fingers trace the outstretched wings of the bird in flight. She remembered what Frau Friedrickson had said of her husband's wedding gift: "Hugo always said my spirit was the thing that first made him love me."

I hope you are together now, Anna thought, as tears began to blur her eyes. *I hope your spirits soar together and that you are happy.*

And someday I hope that you will forgive me, she thought. She wasn't sure she would ever forgive herself.

"Excuse me, Fraulein Becker."

Reaching for a handkerchief to wipe her eyes, Anna shifted to one side at the quiet male voice beside her. She expected whoever it was to move on past her, but he did not. Instead, he stepped even closer, so close as to almost touch her.

"Forgive me," he said again. "But there is not much time left, and I must ask you to listen to me. No, do not turn your head," he went on. This time, Anna could hear the urgency threaded through his voice.

"Continue looking at the coffins, if you please. You have stopped beside Karl Mueller's. He was a friend of yours, was he not? If this is so, please wipe your eyes once more."

Mystified, Anna pressed the handkerchief to her face.

"Thank you, Fraulein Becker," the man continued. "Karl was a friend of mine also, though you do not know me. He asked me to do something for him, something I will honor as his deathbed wish."

"What?" Anna whispered, staring at Karl's coffin now, still not daring to turn her head.

"He asked me to be certain you were not sent back to Germany."

Anna felt the world around her tilt. Her heart pounded so loud that her ears rang with it. She swayed on her feet, then felt an arm reach out to steady her.

"The young lady is feeling unwell," the male voice at her side said. "Please make way."

In a daze, Anna felt herself being piloted swiftly away from the row of coffins. She expected Herr Heiss to appear at any moment, demanding an explanation.

"Herr Heiss," she managed to gasp out.

"Do not concern yourself about Herr Heiss, fraulein," her companion answered, slowing his pace. "He is occupied for the moment."

He turned Anna gently. Through the crowd, she could see Herr Heiss talking to a group of men in German uniforms.

"Fraulein Becker, I must ask you to listen, and to trust me."

For the first time, Anna turned to look at her companion. She was surprised to see he looked vaguely familiar.

"Do I know you?" she asked.

The man smiled briefly. He was older than Anna, about the age her father would have been, she guessed. Dark brown hair waved back from a high forehead. Brown eyes gazed compassionately into Anna's blue ones.

"I am a member of the Lakehurst ground crew," he said. "I was the one who made sure you reached the hospital, Fraulein Becker."

The one whose arms had held her so that she could not hurl herself back into the burning ship, Anna realized suddenly. This man had visited the hospital, too. She recalled him as a quiet presence hovering in the background. Even after Karl's death he had come.

"How did you know Karl?" she asked, her mind swimming. Something was happening, but she could not take it in.

"I grew up with his father," the man answered quietly. "I had a son about Karl's age. After he . . . disappeared . . . Karl helped the rest of my family to come to America. He knew that if ever he needed anything, all he had to do was ask."

"And this is what Karl asked you to do?" Anna asked, still unable to believe what she was hearing. The man nodded, his eyes intent on her face. "When did he ask this?" Anna asked.

Momentary surprise lit the man's features. "But I thought you knew," he said. "Karl's cable came several days ago, the day after you left Germany. He wired me early that morning asking for my help. Saying I must be prepared for someone else to meet you also, someone who would try to take you back to Germany. Karl said he wished he could explain more, but he could not."

"But you are prepared to do this thing he asks?" Anna said. "Even though he gave you no reason?"

Again the man looked surprised. "Of course. Karl was my friend, Fraulein Becker. I took his request on faith, as he would have taken mine."

Anna had thought there was no part of her heart left to break. Now she discovered that she was mistaken.

On faith, she thought. Something she hadn't had in Karl, nor he in her. *Oh, Karl, if only you had told me. If only we'd been honest with each other, right from the beginning.*

He'd never intended to send her back, even when he'd threatened most vehemently to do so. By the time he'd secured her promise of aid during their painful encounter in the smoking room, he had already wired this man to make sure that she would not be sent back to Germany.

The gray mist around Anna was pierced by sudden blinding pain. How could she take what Karl offered, when she'd offered him so little in exchange?

"Your offer is very kind," she said. "But I am not certain I can accept it. I think perhaps it would be better if I returned to Germany." How could she accept life, when Karl was gone forever?

"I do not understand," the man said.

"I killed him," Anna whispered, the words welling up out of her before she could stop them. The horrible knowledge she held inside her had burst its bonds; it could be contained no longer.

"I killed them all. Karl asked for my help, but I would not do for him what you have done. I would not give him my faith. I would not help him. It is only fitting that I should go back to Germany, to the life my brother has chosen for me. But first I should go to the authorities. I should tell them what I know. Sabotage, the *Hindenburg* was sabotaged."

The man grasped her firmly by one elbow. To

stop her desperate flow of words, he gave her arm one sharp shake. "I beg you, Fraulein Becker," he said urgently, "do not say such things. Coming forward will do no good. It could even be dangerous for you."

"But why?" Anna protested.

He gave her arm another little shake. "Think, fraulein," he said. "Do you think the Nazis will thank you? Do you think they will want to admit that sabotage could destroy their great airship, the symbol of their invincibility? They do not wish to do that, will never do that, and if you try to do it, they will stop you. You cannot come forward. You must not. Please, you must believe me."

Anna paused, struck by his answer. What was it Erik had said in those last desperate moments?

"The world must be shown that the Nazis are not invincible."

But would anyone know, if she stayed silent? Would even Erik have died in vain?

"How will I live with myself?" she whispered in anguish. "How will I live, knowing I did nothing?"

"But you will not do nothing, fraulein," her unknown savior answered. "You will do the thing Karl wanted most. You will start a new life in America.

"You alone cannot have been responsible for the destruction of the *Hindenburg*. Others set the plot in motion long before you boarded the airship. If what you say is true and it was sabotage, even if this attempt had failed, another would soon come to take its place."

"But I did not stop it," Anna whispered. "I did not stop it."

"That is not the same as saying you caused it," he answered. "I see how this pains you, Fraulein Becker, and I can offer you no real comfort. I can only remind you that you cannot change the past, and if you live in it, you can never have a future."

Anna stared at him. "I do not even know your name," she said.

The man's mouth lifted in a slight smile. "My apologies. I am Anton Bauer."

Anton, Anna thought. *Oh, Opa, do you hear?*

He had the name of the grandfather who had been her most trusted confidant and of the father she had loved but who had been taken from her far too soon.

And he has lost loved ones, too, she thought, remembering the son that he had mentioned. But Anton Bauer could do what her father and grandfather could not: offer her the chance of a new life.

And unlike Herr Heiss, he could do so without demanding that Anna abandon her grief for all that had and had not happened.

Perhaps I don't have to go back, Anna thought. *Perhaps it is possible to start over*. Her spirit would not soar, not for a long time. But that didn't mean she had to bury it in Karl Mueller's coffin.

For the first time since Karl's death, Anna experienced a feeling she'd thought was gone forever: curiosity.

What will my new life be like? she wondered. *Can I make something of this chance I have been given?*

The chance Karl had given her.

"I am sorry to rush you, Fraulein Becker," Anton Bauer said with a quick glance over his shoulder. "But I must ask you to come with me now, before the crowds thin out and our departure can be noticed. I know I ask a great deal—that you put your trust in a stranger."

But you are not a stranger, Anna thought. *You are Karl's friend, someone he trusted.*

And if she did not trust him now, Anna knew she would stay mired in the past forever. She would throw away Karl's last gift. He would have died for nothing.

Anna's future might be hard. It was bound to be uncertain. But she knew now that fulfilling its promise was up to her.

"You are not a stranger," she said aloud. "I will take you and your family as you take me—on faith, Herr Bauer."

And I won't look back, Anna thought. *I won't ever look back.*

"I am ready to go whenever you are."

A Note from the Author

This is a work of historical fiction, a term which can mean many things. Sometimes it's an entirely made up story, set in a different time period than our own. But in this case, I've created a fictional story based on actual events.

Try thinking of the *Hindenburg* itself, with its rigid metal frame. In my story, the frame is made up of the events we know took place: the *Hindenburg*'s departure from Frankfurt on May 3, 1937, and its fiery destruction three days later. But the thing that gives my story its lift is pure fiction. Anna Becker, Karl Mueller, Erik Peterson, and Frau Friedrickson never flew on the *Hindenburg*. Their stories existed only in my heart and head. Those characters aren't based on real people. (There are times in the story when I've used real names, but portrayed these people in a fictional manner.)

Max Pruss really was the captain of the *Hindenburg* on its last flight. Otto and Else Ernst; Joseph Spah;

his dog, Ulla; and Frau Emilie Imhof, the stewardess, were all real people. Spah and Else Ernst survived the fire. Otto Ernst, Frau Imhof, and Ulla the dog did not.

One published account had Frau Erst sliding down a rope to safety, but another has the Ernsts as a couple staggering down one of the gangways. The supports that held the gangways up during flight burned away during the fire. When that happened, the stairs dropped down just as if the landing were a perfectly normal one. Several passengers simply walked right down them and off the burning airship.

I've always thought the fact that anyone survived at all is nothing less than amazing.

The *Hindenburg* was 804 feet long, larger than any modern jumbo jet, and just 78 feet shorter than the 882 foot oceangoing *Titanic*. How long did it take that enormous length to burn from end to end and fall from the sky?

Just a little over thirty seconds.

Approximately half a minute after the first flame appeared near its tail, all that remained of the *Hindenburg* lay on the landing field at Lakehurst like the twisted skeleton of some enormous metal animal. It was roughly 700 feet away from the mooring mast and safety.

We still don't really know what started the conflagration.

The investigation that followed the disaster came to the conclusion that sabotage was not involved in the *Hindendurg*'s destruction, though rumors of sabotage were rampant at the time and have continued to this day.

Those who suspected sabotage pointed to the fact that the two zeppelins, the *Graf* and the *Hindenburg*, had made more than six hundred flights without mishap. This included being struck by lightning while in flight and landing right after a storm, as the *Hindenburg* attempted to do on May 6, 1937.

These individuals, many of them airmen who felt they knew from personal experience what the great ships could do, considered the zeppelins completely safe in spite of their gas cells filled with hydrogen. They believed that sabotage was the only possible explanation for the sudden destruction of the *Hindenburg*.

But the official explanation was that the "most probable" cause of the disaster was a hydrogen leak in one of the rear gas cells, which was ignited by a spark of static electricity, causing the ship to burst into flames.

In making sabotage responsible for the *Hindenburg*'s destruction in my story, I've chosen the more dramatic of the two options.

The one thing upon which everyone seemed to agree was that the *Hindenburg* would not have burned if it had been filled with helium rather than hydrogen.

During World War I, however, Germany had used earlier rigid airships as part of their war efforts. This may have led American officials in 1937 to have some misgivings about supplying the Germans with helium.

How did they know Germany would not use its airships for military purposes at some time in the future, this time buoyed with something the Americans had provided? The German request for helium was denied, leaving the Zeppelin Company with no choice but to fill its airships with hightly flammable hydrogen.

If you're interested in reading more about the *Hindenburg*, check out *Hindenburg, An Illustrated History* (text by Rich Archbold, paintings by Ken Marschall). This book has great photos of the airship itself, and it also provides a lot of interesting history.

Do you know why the ship is called a zeppelin? Or that the *Hindenburg* was not a blimp, for instance?

Two videos are also available, both called *The Hindenburg*. One is another fictionalized account of the final flight—and, yes, once more, sabotage was chosen as the more dramatic option. The other videotape is nonfiction, another history. This has great shots of early airships and the later zeppelins. It also includes footage of the *Hindenburg* burning and falling to the ground, as well as the live radio broadcast that begins so well, and ends with the broadcaster weeping into the microphone: "Oh, the humanity. . . ."

About the Author

CAMERON DOKEY lives in Seattle, Washington. During the time it took her to write this book, the part of the country in which she lives set a whole new record for total rainfall. She is seriously considering setting her next book on a nice sunny tropical island and then relocating there to write it.

Cameron has one husband and three cats and is the author of twelve novels for young adults. She has also written two short story collections. Her favorite books are the novels in J. R. R. Tolkien's trilogy, *The Lord of the Rings*. Her favorite TV show is *Buffy the Vampire Slayer*.

When she's not writing books, Cameron likes to work in her garden—or she would if it would ever stop raining.

She also knows every weird word in the entire universe that rhymes with her weird last name. So if you're thinking of writing to her about *Hindenburg, 1937* (and she sincerely hopes you will), you can just spare her any funny stuff like "Okey Dokey."

Trust her, she's heard it.

Happy reading!